Ben Bova is the Hugo-winning editor of *Analog* magazine. He is also author of a number of non-fiction and science fiction works including *Millennium* (also available in Orbit).

Novella: 3

3 Novellas
edited by
Ben Bova

Futura Publications Limited
An Orbit Book

An Orbit Book

Edited by Ben Bova
Associate Editors:
Peter Weston and Victoria Schochet

First published in Great Britain by
Futura Publications Limited in 1978

ISBN 0 7088 8015 0

Printed by
William Collins Sons & Co. Ltd
Glasgow

Futura Publications Limited,
110 Warner Road, Camberwell,
London SE5.

CONTENTS

ACKNOWLEDGEMENTS

GIANT KILLER by A. Bertram Chandler
Copyright © 1945 by Street & Smith Publications Inc.
Copyright © 1973 (renewed) by The Conde Nast Publications
Inc.
Reprinted by permission of The Conde Nast Publications Inc.

THE BLACK DESTROYER by A. E. van Vogt
Copyright © 1939 by Street & Smith Publications Inc.
Copyright © 1967 (renewed) by A. E. van Vogt
Reprinted by permission of the author's agent. E. J. Carnell
Literary Agency.

FIREWATER by William Tenn
Copyright © 1952 by Street & Smith Publications Inc.
Reprinted by permission of the author and Henry Morrison
Inc (USA) his agents.

INTRODUCTION

By Ben Bova

Science fiction is booming everywhere, all through the industrialized (and industrializing) nations of the world.

This series of THREE BY anthologies is a part of that boom, an effort to bring to science fiction readers old and new those classic tales that have been too often neglected by anthologists. In this volume we have novellas by A. Bertram Chandler, A. E. van Vogt, and William Tenn (the penname of Philip Klass). These world-renowned writers hardly need an introduction here: their works have been enjoyed by discerning readers for thirty years and more.

It has been my custom to eschew introductions to the individual stories published in this series. Certainly 'Giant Killer', 'The Black Destroyer' and 'Firewater' are perfectly capable of standing on their own, without the need of dubious editorial commentary. Rather, I want to talk about what's happening in the entertainment industry at the moment, because it is important to the consideration of the stories in this book.

Out in sunny-smoggy Hollywood, the millennium has arrived early. Science fiction is now big business in the entertainment industry. And Hollywood isn't the only entertainment-industry centre where science fiction has become a colossus. Long lines of ticket buyers are circling cinemas all over North America, Great Britain and Europe to see STAR WARS. Dozens of science fiction shows are already on television in the United States, or in production for next season. The $18-million CLOSE ENCOUNTERS OF THE THIRD KIND generated enormous interest around the world even before it reached the cinemas.

Grown adults have gone to see STAR WARS eight or nine times. American university students halt their studies faithfully every day to watch the fiftieth re-run of STAR TREK episodes on TV. Even the stock market has been affected by science fiction films: Twentieth Century Fox's stock soared as STAR WARS took the world by storm; Columbia's stock sagged when the first sneak previews of CLOSE EN-COUNTERS received responses that were less than ecstatic.

What's going on here? How can *science fiction*, of all things, become Important? What makes otherwise sane people spend a healthy slice of their salaries to see a film like STAR WARS a half-dozen times?

Psychologists and social thinkers are bending their pet theories into pretzels to account for the so-called 'science fiction phenomenon'. But to veteran science fictioneers, there appear to be three major reasons for the new-found success of SF in the cinema.

(And please note that it is abbreviated 'SF', not 'sci-fi', a linguistic barbarism used only by ignorant disc jockeys and desperate headline writers.)

The first reason for science fiction's booming popularity is *excitement*. In an era where almost every new film is a remake of an earlier film, science fiction offers bold new visions for jaded audiences. SF has a 'sense of wonder'. With all of the starry universe and all of time to play in, science fiction spreads a huge canvas, on which are painted stories of epic scope and sweep, like 'The Black Destroyer'. It would be impossible to tell this kind of tale outside of the science fiction field.

The second reason is something that can best be termed *morality*. We think we're too sophisticated for old-fashioned virtues such as honesty and courage. But the basic concepts of good and evil still underlie every tale, and in science fiction the good guys are usually easy to distinguish from the bad guys. The cinema audience is encouraged to act on its simple, fundamental instincts, cheering for the hero and hissing the villain. And as Al Capp's Mammy Yokum often put it, 'Good always triumphs over evil – 'cause it's nicer'.

We can find supporting evidence for this moral attitude from a completely different aspect of 'show business'. Whenever NASA launches a large rocket, there are many 'religious conversions' in the crowds of onlookers. Men and women who merely came to see the launch because they were curious return home with newfound fervor for space exploration. Something about those thundering, blazing, awe-inspiring rocket lift-off's literally inspires people to something akin to a religious revelation. I have seen skeptics turned into devoted evangelists, in the time it takes to go from 'ignition' to 'first stage burnout'.

People want something to believe in, whether it's the correctness of exploring outer space, or the conviction that the good guys must and will beat the bad guys – even if it's only on film.

The third reason for the burgeoning popularity of SF films is the public's growing *concern about the future.* Call it Future Shock, Technology Assessment, or whatever, we are now a future-oriented society. We demonstrate against SST's, nuclear powerplants, recombinant DNA experiments because of the damage they might do in the future.

Science fiction films show the public the future – or at least, glimpses of what some possible futures might be like. Certainly, these films are not meant to be predictions or even guesses about what our future might truly be. But they do take the audience out of the here-and-now and show worlds that are totally different from our own.

Escapism ? Of course. But as Isaac Asimov has said, science fiction is 'escape into reality.' Instead of watching Fred Astaire and Ginger Rogers dance their way through the Depression, we are now seeing films that hammer home the theme of *change,* the concept that tomorrow will be vastly different from today.

All this makes science fiction a film-maker's dream: panoramic excitement, strongly moralistic stories, exotic backgrounds and spectacular visual effects. Small wonder that directors such as Steven Spielberg and George Lucas have turned to science fiction.

Interestingly, both Lucas and Spielberg (as well as Gene Roddenberry, the creator of STAR TREK) were SF readers as teenagers. Spielberg made an amateur science fiction film when he was 16. Lucas' THX 1138 was first an undergraduate project when he was at UCLA and only later was expanded into a commercial film for Warner's.

We are seeing, then, the results of a new generation of film-makers who grew up reading science fiction and accepting it as a perfectly valid literature for their times.

As a distinct literary field, science fiction is just over fifty years old. The first magazine to specialize in science fiction, *Amazing Stories*, began publication in the U.S. in 1926. Two generations of readers have slowly but continuously added to the ranks of SF lovers, until today there are millions of people around the world who have been reading science fiction since childhood.

Science fiction is not easy reading. It demands much of the reader. Published science fiction (as distinct from SF in films) is deliberately intended to challenge the reader's unconscious assumptions and prejudices. It is intended to force the reader to think, to question, to open his or her mind to new vistas of thought. It is a literature aimed at the relatively small number of readers who enjoy thinking.

With depressingly rare exceptions, science fiction in the cinema or on TV has gone the other way. Films and TV productions must, by the nature of their economics, be aimed at mass audiences. Where a science fiction novel can be a commercial success with 100,000 paperback sales, a science fiction film must play to tens of millions of viewers, or go broke.

This means that heavy thinking, challenges to the audience's brains, are usually taboo in SF films. Producers go for spectacular special effects, weird-looking aliens, and skimpy skirts on the women.

Once every decade or so, a dedicated team of movie makers will bring out a film such as the Kubrick–Clarke classic 2001: A SPACE ODYSSEY, or CHARLIE (the only SF film to date in which the leading actor, Cliff Robertson, received an Academy Award), or THE MAN IN THE WHITE SUIT, from Ealing Studios, which starred Alec Guiness. These are films that delight the eye *and* the mind.

Neither Spielberg nor Lucas has attempted to do this much, as yet. And neither of them calls his film science fiction.

Spielberg says that CLOSE ENCOUNTERS is an 'adventure thriller'. Lucas describes STAR WARS as 'space fantasy'. No doubt both of them realize that their films fall far, far short of the intellectual excitement and challenge to be found in the best science fiction stories.

Both CLOSE ENCOUNTERS and STAR WARS draw on science fiction themes that date back to the 1930s: invasion of Earth by alien intelligences, and old-fashioned 'space opera', complete with flashing rayguns and dashing interstellar spaceships.

There will be a galaxy of new science fiction films as a result of the successes of STAR WARS and CLOSE ENCOUNTERS. Most of these films will also be firmly imbedded in the 'Blood and Thunder' tradition of science fiction's younger years.

But maybe, if we are very, very lucky, intelligent directors such as Spielberg and Lucas will work up the courage to try some of the best SF from later years: perhaps someday they might even try to film 'Firewater', or 'Giant Killer', or 'The Black Destroyer'.

That will be worth looking for!

Ben Bova
Manhattan
1978

GIANT KILLER

by A. Bertram Chandler

We've read of mutant supermen, of strange and alien races on other worlds. But never have we had a tale of quite so homely, yet so utterly alien a race, nor of quite such a super-mutant. Chandler has a yarn to tell –

Shrick should have died before his baby eyes had opened on his world. Shrick would have died, but Weena, his mother, was determined that he, alone of all her children, should live. Three previous times since her mating with Skreer had she borne, and on each occasion the old, gray Sterrett, Judge of the Newborn, had condemned her young as Different Ones.

Weena had no objection to the Law when it did not affect her or hers. She, as much as any other member of the Tribe, keenly enjoyed the feasts of fresh, tasty meat following the ritual slaughter of the Different Ones. But when those sacrificed were the fruit of her own womb it wasn't the same.

It was quiet in the cave where Weena awaited the coming of her lord. Quiet, that is, save for the sound of her breathing and an occasional plaintive, mewling cry from the newborn child. And even these sounds were deadened by the soft spongy walls and ceiling.

She sensed the coming of Skreer long before his actual arrival. She anticipated his first question and, as he entered the cave, said quietly, 'One. A male.'

'A male?' Skreer radiated approval. Then she felt his mood change to one of questioning, of doubt. 'Is it . . . he – ?'

'Yes.'

Skreer caught the tiny, warm being in his arms. There was no light, but he, like all his race, was accustomed to the dark. His fingers told him all that he needed to know. The child was

12

hairless. The legs were too straight. And – this was worst of all – the head was a great, bulging dome.

'Skreer!' Weena's voice was anxious. 'Do you – ?'

'There is no doubt. Sterret will condemn it as a Different One.'

'But –'

'There is no hope.' Weena sensed that her mate shuddered, heard the faint, silken rustle of his fur as he did so. 'His head! He is like the Giants!'

The mother sighed. It was hard, but she knew the Law. And yet – This was her fourth child-bearing, and she was never to know, perhaps, what it was to watch and wait with mingled pride and terror whilst her sons set out with the other young males to raid the Giants' territory, to bring back spoils from the great Cave-of-Food, the Place-of-Green-Growing-Things or, even, precious scraps of shiny metal from the Place-of-Life-That-Is-Not-Life.

She clutched at a faint hope.

'His head is like a Giant's? Can it be, do you think, that the Giants are Different Ones? I have heard it said.'

'What if they are?'

'Only this. Perhaps he will grow to be a Giant. Perhaps he will fight the other Giants for us, his own people. Perhaps –'

'Perhaps Sterret will let him live, you mean.' Skreer made the short, unpleasant sound that passed among his people for a laugh. 'No, Weena. He must die. And it is long since we feasted –'

'But –'

'Enough. Or do *you* wish to provide meat for the Tribe also? I may wish to find a mate who will bear me sturdy sons, not monsters!'

The Place-of-Meeting was almost deserted when Skreer and Weena, she with Shrick clutched tightly in her arms, entered. Two more couples were there, each with newborn. One of the mothers was holding two babies, each of whom appeared to be normal. The other had three, her mate holding one of them.

Weena recognized her as Teeza, and flashed her a little half

13

smile of sympathy when she saw that the child carried by Teeza's mate would certainly be condemned by Sterret when he chose to appear. For it was, perhaps, even more revolting than her own Different One, having two hands growing from the end of each arm.

Skreer approached one of the other males, he unburdened with a child.

'How long have you been waiting?' he asked.

'Many heartbeats. We –'

The guard stationed at the doorway through which light entered from Inside hissed a warning:

'Quiet! A Giant is coming!'

The mothers clutched their children to them yet more tightly, their fur standing on end with superstitious dread. They knew that if they remained silent there was no danger, that even if they should betray themselves by some slight noise there was no immediate peril. It was not size alone that made the Giants dreaded, it was the supernatural powers that they were known to possess. The food-that-kills had slain many an unwary member of the tribe, also their fiendishly cunning devices that crushed and mangled any of the People unwise enough to reach greedily for the savory morsels left exposed on a kind of little platform. Although there were those who averred that, in the latter case, the risk was well worth it, for the yellow grains from the many bags in the Cave-of-Food were as monotonous as they were nourishing.

'The Giant has passed!'

Before those in the Place-of-Meeting could resume their talk, Sterret drifted out from the entrance of his cave. He held in his right hand his wand of office, a straight staff of the hard, yet soft, stuff dividing the territory of the People from that of the Giants. It was tipped with a sharp point of metal.

He was old, was Sterret.

Those who were themselves grandparents had heard their grandparents speak of him. For generations he had survived attacks by young males jealous of his prerogatives as chief, and the more rare assaults by parents displeased by his rulings as Judge of the Newborn. In this latter case, however, he had had nothing to fear, for on those isolated occasions the tribe had risen as one and torn the offenders to pieces.

Behind Sterret came his personal guards and then, floating out from the many cave entrances, the bulk of the Tribe. There had been no need to summon them; they *knew*.

The chief, deliberate and unhurried, took his position in the center of the Place-of-Meeting. Without orders, the crowd made way for the parents and their newborn. Weena winced as she saw their gloating eyes fixed on Shrick's revolting baldness, his misshapen skull. She knew what the verdict would be.

She hoped that the newborn of the others would be judged before her own, although that would merely delay the death of her own child by the space of a very few heartbeats. She hoped –

'Weena! Bring the child to me that I may see and pass judgment!'

The chief extended his skinny arms, took the child from the mother's reluctant hands. His little, deep-set eyes gleamed at the thought of the draught of rich, red blood that he was soon to enjoy. And yet he was reluctant to lose the savor of a single heartbeat of the mother's agony. Perhaps she could be provoked into an attack –

'You insult us,' he said slowly, 'by bringing forth *this*!' He held Shrick, who squalled feebly, at arm's length. 'Look, oh People, at this *thing* the miserable Weena has brought for my judgment!'

'He has a Giant's head,' Weena's timid voice was barely audible. 'Perhaps –'

'– his father was a Giant!'

A tittering laugh rang through the Place-of-Meeting.

'No. But I have heard it said that perhaps the Giants, or their fathers and mothers, were Different Ones. And –'

'Who said that?'

'Strela.'

'Yes, Strela the Wise. Who, in his wisdom, ate largely of the food-that-kills!'

Again the hateful laughter rippled through the assembly.

Sterret raised the hand that held the spear, shortening his grip on the haft. His face puckered as he tasted in anticipation the bright bubble of blood that would soon well from the throat of the Different One. Weena screamed. With one hand she snatched her child from the hateful grasp of the chief, with the other she seized his spear.

Sterret was old, and generations of authority had made him careless. Yet, old as he was, he evaded the vicious thrust aimed at him by the mother. He had no need to cry orders, from all sides the People converged upon the rebel.

Already horrified by her action, Weena knew that she could expect no mercy. And yet life, even as lived by the Tribe, was sweet. Gaining a purchase from the gray, spongy floor of the Place-of-Meeting she jumped. The impetus of her leap carried her up to the doorway through which streamed the light from inside. The guard there was unarmed, for of what avail would a puny spear be against the Giants? He fell back before the menace of Weena's bright blade and bared teeth. And then Weena was Inside.

She could, she knew, hold the doorway indefinitely against pursuit. But this was Giant country. In an agony of indecision she clung to the rim of the door with one hand, the other still holding the spear. A face appeared in the opening, and then vanished, streaming with blood. It was only later that she realized that it had been Skreer's.

She became acutely conscious of the fierce light beating around and about her, of the vast spaces on all sides of a body that was accustomed to the close quarters of the caves and tunnels. She felt naked and, in spite of her spear, utterly defenceless.

Then that which she dreaded came to pass.

Behind her, she sensed the approach of two of the Giants. Then she could hear their breathing, and the low, infinitely menacing rumble of their voices as they talked one with the other. They hadn't seen her – of that she was certain but it was only a matter of heartbeats before they did so. The open doorway, with the certainty of death that lay beyond, seemed infinitely preferable to the terror of the unknown. Had it been only her life at stake she would have returned to face the righteous wrath of her chief, her mate and her Tribe.

Fighting down her blind panic, she forced herself to a clarity of thought normally foreign to her nature. If she yielded to instinct, if she fled madly before the approaching Giants, she would be seen. Her only hope was to remain utterly still. Skreer, and others of the males who had been on forays Inside, had told her that the Giants, careless in their size and power, more often than not did not notice the people unless they made some betraying movement.

The Giants were very close.

Slowly, cautiously, she turned her head.

She could see them now, two enormous figures floating through the air with easy arrogance. They had not seen her, and she knew that they would not see her unless she made some sudden movement to attract their attention. Yet it was hard not to yield to the impulse to dive back into the doorway to the Place-of-Meeting, there to meet certain death at the hands of the outraged Tribe. It was harder still to fight the urge to relinquish her hold on the rim of the doorway and flee – anywhere – in screaming panic.

But she held on.

The Giants passed.

The dull rumble of their voices died in the distance, their acrid, unpleasant odor, of which she had heard but never before experienced, diminished. Weena dared to raise her head once more.

In the confused, terrified welter of her thoughts one idea stood out with dreadful clarity. Her only hope of survival, pitifully slim though it was, lay in following the Giants. There was no time to lose, already she could hear the rising clamor of voices as those in the caves sensed that the Giants had passed. She relinquished her hold on the edge of the door and floated slowly up.

When Weena's head came into sudden contact with something

17

hard she screamed. For long seconds she waited, eyes closed shut in terror, for the doom that would surely descend upon her. But nothing happened. The pressure upon the top of her skull neither increased nor diminished.

Timidly, she opened her eyes.

As far as she could see, in two directions, stretched a long, straight shaft or rod. Its thickness was that of her own body, and it was made, or covered with, a material not altogether strange to the mother. It was like the ropes woven by the females with fibers from the Place-of-Green-Growing-Things – but incomparably finer. Stuff such as this was brought back sometimes by the males from their expeditions. It had been believed, once, that it was the fur of the Giants, but now it was assumed that it was made by them for their own purposes.

On three sides of the shaft was the glaring emptiness so terrifying to the people of the caves. On the fourth side was a flat, shiny surface. Weena found that she could insinuate herself into the space between the two without discomfort. She discovered, also, that with comforting solidity at her back and belly she could make reasonably fast progress along the shaft. It was only when she looked to either side that she felt a return of her vertigo. She soon learned not to look.

It is hard to estimate the time taken by her journey in a world where time was meaningless. Twice she had to stop and feed Shrick – fearful lest his hungry wailings betray their presence either to Giants or any of the People who might – although this was highly improbable – have followed her. Once she felt the shaft vibrating, and froze to its matt surface in utter and abject terror. A Giant passed, pulling himself rapidly along with his two hands. Had either of those hands fallen upon Weena it would have been the finish. For many heart-beats after his passing she clung there limp and helpless, scarcely daring to breath.

It seemed that she passed through places of which she had heard the males talk. This may have been so – but she had no means of knowing. For the world of the People, with its caves and tunnels, was familiar territory, whilst that of the Giants was known only in relation to the doorways through which a daring explorer could enter.

Weena was sick and faint with hunger and thirst when, at last, the long shaft led her into a place where she could smell the tantilizing aroma of food. She stopped, looked in all directions. But here, as everywhere in this alien country, the light was too dazzling for her untrained eyes. She could see, dimly, vast shapes beyond her limited understanding. She could see no Giants, nor anything that moved.

Cautiously, keeping a tight hold on the rough surface of the shaft, she edged out to the side away from the polished, flat surface along which she had been traveling. Back and forth her head swung, her sensitive nostrils dilated. The bright light confused her, so she shut her eyes. Once again her nose sought the source of the savory smell, swinging ever more slowly as the position was determined with reasonable accuracy.

She was loath to abandon the security of her shaft, but hunger overruled all other considerations. Orienting her body, she jumped. With a thud she brought up against another flat surface. Her free hand found a projection, to which she clung. This she almost relinquished as it turned. Then a crack appeared, with disconcerting suddenness, before her eyes, widening rapidly. Behind this opening was black, welcome darkness. Weena slipped inside, grateful for relief from the glaring light of the Inside. It wasn't until later that she realized that this was a door such as was made by her own people in the Barrier, but a door of truly gigantic proportions. But all that mattered at first was the cool, refreshing shade.

Then she took stock of her surroundings.

Enough light came in through the barely open doorway for her to see that she was in a cave. It was the wrong shape for a cave, it is true, having flat, perfectly regular walls and floor and ceiling. At the far end, each in its own little compartment, were enormous, dully shining globes. From them came a smell that almost drove the famishing mother frantic.

Yet she held back. She knew that smell. It was that of fragments of food that had been brought into the caves, won by stealth and guile from the killing platforms of the Giants. Was this a killing platform? She racked her brains to recall the poor description of these devices given by the males, decided that this, after all, must be a Cave-of-Food. Relinquishing her hold of Shrick and Sterret's spear she made for the nearest globe.

At first she tried to pull it from its compartment, but it appeared to be held. But it didn't matter. Bringing her face against the surface of the sphere she buried her teeth in its thin skin. There was flesh beneath the skin, and blood – a thin, sweet, faintly acid juice. Skreer had, at times, promised her a share of this food when next he won some from a killing platform, but that promise had never been kept. And now Weena had a whole cave of this same food all to herself.

Gorged to repletion, she started back to pick up the now loudly complaining Shrick. He had been playing with the spear and had cut himself on the sharp point. But it was the spear that Weena snatched, swinging swiftly to defend herself and her child. For a voice said, understandable, but with an oddly slurred intonation, 'Who are you? What are you doing in our country?'

It was one of the People, a male. He was unarmed, otherwise it is certain that he would never have asked questions. Even so, Weena knew that the slightest relaxation of vigilance on her part would bring a savage tooth and nail attack.

She tightened her grasp on the spear, swung it so that its point was directed at the stranger.

'I am Weena,' she said, 'of the Tribe of Sterrett.'

'Of the Tribe of Sterrett? But the Tribe of Sessa holds the ways between our countries.'

'I came Inside. But who are you?'

'Tekka. I am one of Skarro's people. You are a spy.'

'So I brought my child with me.'

Tekka was looking at Shrick.

'I see,' he said at last. 'A Different One. But how did you get through Sessa's country?'

'I didn't. I came Inside.'

It was obvious that Tekka refused to believe her story.

'You must come with me,' he said, 'to Skarro. He will

judge.'

'And if I come?'

'For the Different One, death. For you, I do not know. But we have too many females in our Tribe already.'

'This says that I will not come.' Weena brandished her spear.

She would not have defied a male of her own tribe thus – but this Tekka was not of her people. And she had always been brought up to believe that even a female of the Tribe of Sterrett was superior to a male – even a chief – of any alien community.

'The Giants will find you here.' Tekka's voice showed an elaborate unconcern. Then – 'That is a fine spear.'

'Yes. It belonged to Sterrett. With it I wounded my mate. Perhaps he is dead.'

The male looked at her with a new respect. If her story were true – this was a female to be handled with caution. Besides –

'Would you give it to me?'

'Yes.' Weena laughed nastily. There was no mistaking her meaning.

'Not that way. Listen. Not long ago, in our Tribe, many mothers, two whole hands of mothers with Different Ones, defied the Judge of the Newborn. They fled along the tunnels, and live outside the Place-of-Little-Lights. Skarro has not yet led a war party against them. Why, I do not know, but there is always a Giant in that place. It may be that Skarro fears that a fight behind the Barrier would warn the Giants of our presence –'

'And you will lead me there?'

'Yes. In return for the spear.'

Weena was silent for the space of several heartbeats. As long as Tekka preceded her she would be safe. It never occurred to her that she could let the other fulfill his part of the bargain, and then refuse him his payment. Her people were a very primitive race.

'I will come with you,' she said.

'It is well.'

Tekka's eyes dwelt long and lovingly upon the fine spear.

Skarro would not be chief much longer.

'First,' he said, 'we must pull what you have left of the good-to-eat-ball into our tunnel. Then I must shut the door lest a Giant should come–'

Together they hacked and tore the sphere to pieces. There was a doorway at the rear of one of the little compartments, now empty. Through this they pushed and pulled their fragrant burden. First Weena went into the tunnel, carrying Shrick and the spear, then Tekka. He pushed the round door into place, where it fitted with no sign that the Barrier had been broken. He pushed home two crude locking bars.

'Follow me,' he ordered the mother.

The long journey through the caves and tunnels was heaven after the Inside. Here there was no light – or, at worse, only a feeble glimmer from small holes and cracks in the Barrier. It seemed that Tekka was leading her along the least frequented ways and tunnels of Skarro's country, for they met none of his people. Nevertheless, Weena's perceptions told her that she was in densely populated territory. From all around her beat the warm, comforting waves of the routine, humdrum life of the People. She knew that in snug caves males, females and children were living in cozy intimacy. Briefly she regretted having thrown away all this for the ugly, hairless bundle in her arms. But she could never return to her own Tribe, and should she wish to throw in her lot with this alien community the alternatives would be death or slavery.

'Careful!' hissed Tekka. 'We are approaching Their country.'

'You will – ?'

'Not me. They will kill me. Just keep straight along this tunnel and you will find Them. Now, give me the spear.'

'But –'

'*You* are safe. There is your pass.' He lightly patted the uneasy, squirming Shrick. 'Give me the spear, and I will go.'

Reluctantly, Weena handed over the weapon. Without a word Tekka took it. Then he was gone. Briefly the mother saw him in the dim light that, in this part of the tunnel, filtered through the Barrier – a dim, gray figure rapidly losing itself in the dim grayness. She felt very lost and lonely and frightened. But the die was cast. Slowly, cautiously, she began to creep along the tunnel.

When They found her she screamed. For many heartbeats she had sensed their hateful presence, had felt that beings even more alien than the Giants were closing in on her. Once or twice she called, crying that she came in peace, that she was the mother of a Different One. But not even echo answered her, for the soft, spongy tunnel walls deadened the shrill sound of her voice. And the silence that was not silence was, if that were possible, more menacing than before.

Without warning the stealthy terror struck. Weena fought with the courage of desperation, but she was overcome by sheer weight of numbers. Shrick, protesting feebly, was torn from her frantic grasp. Hands – and surely there were far too many hands for the number of her assailants – pinned her arms to her sides, held her ankles in a vice-like grip. No longer able to struggle she looked at her captors. Then she screamed again. Mercifully, the dim light spared her the full horror of their appearance, but what she saw would have been enough to haunt her dreams to her dying day had she escaped.

Softly, almost caressingly, the hateful hands ran over her body with disgusting intimacy.

Then – 'She is a Different One.'

She allowed herself to hope.

'And the child ?'

'Two-Tails has newborn. She can nurse him.'

And as the sharp blade found her throat Weena had time to regret most bitterly ever having left her snug, familiar world. It was not so much the forfeit of her own life – that she had sacrificed when she defied Sterrett – it was the knowledge that Shrick, instead of meeting a clean death at the hands of his own people, would live out his life among these unclean monstrosities.

Then there was a sharp pain and a feeling of utter helplessness as the tide of her life swiftly ebbed – and the darkness that

Weena had loved so well closed about her for evermore.

No-Fur – who, at his birth, had been named Shrick – fidgetted impatiently at his post midway along what was known to his people as Skarro's Tunnel. It was time that Long-Nose came to relieve him. Many heartbeats had passed since he had heard the sounds on the other side of the Barrier proclaiming that the Giant in the Place-of-Little-Lights had been replaced by another of his kind. It was a mystery what the Giants did there – but the New People had come to recognize a strange regularity in the actions of the monstrous beings, and to regulate their time accordingly.

No-Fur tightened his grip on his spear – of Barrier material it was, roughly sharpened at one end – as he sensed the approach of somebody along the tunnel, coming from the direction of Tekka's country. It could be a Different One bearing a child who would become one of the New People, it could be attack. But, somehow, the confused impressions that his mind received did not bear out either of these assumptions.

No-Fur shrank against the wall of the tunnel, his body sinking deep into the spongy material. Now he could dimly see the intruder – a solitary form flitting furtively through the shadows. His sense of smell told him that it was a female. Yet he was certain that she had no child with her. He tensed himself to attack as soon as the stranger should pass his hiding place.

Surprisingly, she stopped.

'I come in peace,' she said. 'I am one of you. I am,' here she paused a little, 'one of the New People.'

Shrick made no reply, no betraying movement. It was barely possible, he knew, that this female might be possessed of abnormally keen eyesight. It was even more likely that she had smelled him out. But then – how was it that she had known the name by which the New People called themselves? To the outside world they were Different Ones – and had the stranger called herself such she would at once have proclaimed herself an alien whose life was forfeit.

'You do not know,' the voice came again, 'how it is that I

24

called myself by the proper name. In my own Tribe I am called a Different One –'

'Then how is it,' No-Fur's voice was triumphant, 'that you were allowed to live?'

'Come to me! No, leave your spear. Now come!'

No-Fur stuck his weapon into the soft cavern wall. Slowly, almost fearfully, he advanced to where the female was waiting. He could see her better now – and she seemed no different from those fugitive mothers of Different Ones – at whose slaughter he had so often assisted. The body was well proportioned and covered with fine, silky fur. The head was well shaped. Physically she was so normal as to seem repugnant to the New People.

And yet – No-Fur found himself comparing her with the females of his own Tribe, to the disadvantage of the latter. Emotion rather than reason told him that the hatred inspired by the sight of an ordinary body was the result of a deep-rooted feeling of inferiority rather than anything else. And he wanted this stranger.

'No,' she said slowly, 'it is not my body that is different. It is in my head. I didn't know myself until a little while – about two hands of feeding – ago. But I can tell, now, what is going on inside your head, or the head of any of the People –'

'But,' asked the male, 'how did they –'

'I was ripe for mating. I was mated to Trillo, the son of Tekka, the chief. And in our cave I told Trillo things of which he only knew. I thought that I should please him, I thought that he would like to have a mate with magical powers that he could put to good use. With my aid he could have made himself chief. But he was angry – and very frightened. He ran to Tekka, who judged me as a Different One. I was to have been killed, but I was able to escape. They dare not follow me too far into this country –'

Then – 'You want me.'

It was a statement rather than a question.

'Yes. But –'

'No-Tail? She can die. If I fight her and win, I become your mate.'

Briefly, half regretfully, No-Fur thought of his female. She had been patient, she had been loyal. But he saw that, with this stranger for a mate there were no limits to his advancement. It was not that he was more enlightened than Trillo had been, it was that as one of the New People he regarded abnormality as the norm.

'Then you will take me.' Once again there was no hint of questioning. Then – 'My name is Wesel.'

The arrival of No-Fur, with Wesel in tow, at the Place-of-Meeting could not have been better timed. There was a trial in progress, a young male named Big-Ears having been caught red-handed in the act of stealing a coveted piece of metal from the cave of one Four-Arms. Long-Nose, who should have relieved No-Fur, had found the spectacle of a trial with the prospect of a feast to follow far more engrossing than the relief of the lonely sentry.

It was he who first noticed the newcomers.

'Oh, Big-Tusk,' he called, 'No-Fur has deserted his post!'

The chief was disposed to be lenient.

'He has a prisoner,' he said. 'A Different One. We shall feast well.'

'*He is afraid of you,*' hissed Wesel. '*Defy him !*'

'It is no prisoner.' No-Fur's voice was arrogant. 'It is my new mate. And you, Long-Nose, go at once to the tunnel.'

'Go, Long-Nose. My country must not remain unguarded. No-Fur, hand the strange female over to the guards that she may be slaughtered.'

No-Fur felt his resolution wavering under the stern glare of the chief. As two of Big-Tusk's bullies approached he slackened his grip on Wesel's arm. She turned to him, pleading and desperation in her eyes.

'No, no. He is afraid of you, I say. Don't give in to him. Together we can –'

Ironically, it was No-Tail's intervention that turned the scales. She confronted her mate, scorn written on her large unbeautiful face, the shrewish tongue dreaded by all the New People, even the chief himself, fast getting under way.

'So,' she said, 'you prefer this drab, common female to me. Hand her over, so that she may, at least, fill our bellies. As for you, my bucko, you will pay for this insult!'

No-Fur looked at the grotesque, distorted form of No-Tail, and then at the slim, sleek Wesel. Almost without volition he spoke.

'Wesel is my mate,' he said. 'She is one of the New People!'

Big-Tusk lacked the vocabulary to pour adequate scorn upon the insolent rebel. He struggled for words, but could find none to cover the situation. His little eyes gleamed redly, and his hideous tusks were bared in a vicious snarl.

'*Now!*' prompted the stranger. 'His head is confused. He will be rash. His desire to tear and maul will cloud his judgment. Attack!'

No-Fur went into the fight coldly, knowing that if he kept his head he must win. He raised his spear to stem the first rush of the infuriated chief. Just in time Big-Tusk saw the rough point and, using his tail as a rudder, swerved. He wasn't fast enough, although his action barely saved him from immediate death. The spear caught him in the shoulder and broke off short, leaving the end in the wound. Mad with rage and pain the chief was now a most dangerous enemy – and yet, at the same time, easy meat for an adversary who kept his head.

No-Fur was, at first, such a one. But his self-control was cracking fast. Try as he would he could not fight down the rising tides of hysterical fear, of sheer, animal blood lust. As the enemies circled, thrust and parried, he with his almost useless weapon, Big-Tusk with a fine, metal tipped spear, it took all his will power to keep himself from taking refuge in flight or closing to grapple with his more powerful antagonist. His reason told him that both courses of action would be disastrous – the first would end in his being hunted down and slaughtered by the Tribe, the second would bring him within range of the huge, murderous teeth that had given Big-Tusk his name.

So he thrust and parried, thrust and parried, until the keen edge of the chief's blade nicked his arm. The stinging pain made him all animal, and with a shrill scream of fury he

27

launched himself at the other.

But if Nature had provided Big-Tusk with a fine armory she had not been niggardly with the rebel's defensive equipment. True, he had nothing outstanding in the way of teeth or claws, had not the extra limbs possessed by so many of his fellow New People. His brain may have been a little more nimble – but at this stage of the fight that counted for nothing. What saved his life was his hairless skin.

Time after time the chief sought to pull him within striking distance, time after time he pulled away. His slippery hide was crisscrossed with a score of scratches, many of them deep but none immediately serious. And all the time he himself was scratching and pummeling with both hands and feet, biting and gouging.

It seemed that Big-Tusk was tiring, but he was tiring too. And the other had learned that it was useless to try to grab a handful of fur, that he must try to take his enemy in an unbreakable embrace. Once he succeeded. No-Fur was pulled closer and closer to the slavering fangs, felt the foul breath of the other in his face, knew that it was a matter of heartbeats before his throat was torn out. He screamed, threw up his legs and lunged viciously at Big-Tusk's belly. He felt his feet sink into the soft flesh, but the chief grunted and did not relax his pressure. Worse – the failure of his desperate counterattack had brought No-Fur even closer to death.

With one arm, his right, he pushed desperately against the other's chest. He tried to bring his knees up in a crippling blow, but they were held in a vicelike grip by Big-Tusk's heavily muscled legs. With his free, left arm he flailed viciously and desperately, but he might have been beating against the Barrier itself.

The People, now that the issue of the battle was decided, were yelling encouragement to the victor. No-Fur heard among the cheers the voice of his mate, No-Tail. The little, cold corner of his brain in which reason was still enthroned told him that he couldn't blame her. If she were vociferous in *his* support, she could expect only death at the hands of the triumphant chief. But he forgot that he had offered her insult and humiliation, remembered only that she was his mate. And the bitterness of it kept him fighting when others would have relinquished their hold on a life already forfeit.

The edge of his hand came down hard just where Big-Tusk's thick neck joined his shoulder. He was barely conscious that the other winced, the little whimper of pain followed the blow. Then, high and shrill, he heard Wesel.

'Again! Again! That is his weak spot!'

Blindly groping, he searched for the same place. And Big-Tusk was afraid, of that there was no doubt. His head twisted, trying to cover his vulnerability. Again he whimpered, and No-Fur knew that the battle was his. His thin, strong fingers with their sharp nails dug and gouged. There was no fur here, and the flesh was soft. He felt the warm blood welling beneath his hand as the chief screamed dreadfully. Then the iron grip was abruptly relaxed. Before Big-Tusk could use hands or feet to cast his enemy from him No-Fur had twisted and, each hand clutching skin and fur, had buried his teeth in the other's neck. They found the jugular. Almost at once the chief's last, desperate struggles ceased.

No-Fur drank long and satisfyingly.

Then, the blood still clinging to his muzzle, he wearily surveyed the People.

'I am chief,' he said.

'You are the chief!' came back the answering chorus.

'And Wesel is my mate.'

This time there was hesitation on the part of the People. The new chief heard mutters of *'The feast . . . Big-Tusk is old and tough. . . . are we to be cheated –.'*

'Wesel is my mate,' he repeated. Then – 'There is your feast –'

At the height of his power he was to remember No-Tail's stricken eyes, the dreadful feeling that by his words he had put himself outside all custom, all law.

'*Above* the Law,' whispered Wesel.

He steeled his heart.

'There is your feast,' he said again.

29

It was Big-Ears who, snatching a spear from one of the guards, with one swift blow dispatched the cringing No-Tail.

'I am your mate,' said Wesel.

No-Fur took her in his arms. They rubbed noses. It wasn't the old chief's blood that made her shudder ever so slightly. It was the feel of the disgusting, hairless body against her own.

Already the People were carving and dividing the two corpses and wrangling over an even division of the succulent spoils.

There was one among the New People who, had her differences from the racial stock been only psychological, would have been slaughtered long since. Her three eyes notwithstanding, the imprudent exercise of her gift would have brought certain doom. But, like her sisters in more highly civilized communities, she was careful to tell those who came to her only that which they desired to hear. Even then, she exercised restraint. Experience had taught her that foreknowledge of coming events on the part of the participants often resulted in entirely unforeseen results. This annoyed her. Better misfortune on the main stream of Time than well-being on one of its branches.

To this Three-Eyes came No-Fur and Wesel.

Before the chief could ask his questions the seeress raised one emaciated hand.

'You are Shrick,' she said. 'So your mother called you. Shrick, the Giant Killer.'

'But –'

'Wait. You came to ask me about your war against Tekka's people. Continue with your plans. You will win. You will then fight the Tribe of Sterrett the Old. Again you will win. You will be Lord of the Outside. And then –'

'And then ?'

'The Giants will know of the People. Many, but not all, of the People will die. You will fight the Giants. And the last of the Giants you will kill, but he will plunge the world into – Oh, if I could make you see! But we have no words.'

'What – ?'

30

'No, you cannot know. You will never know till the end is upon you. But this I can tell you. The People are doomed. Nothing you or they can do will save them. But you will kill those who will kill us, and that is good.'

Again No-Fur pleaded for enlightenment. Abruptly, his pleas became threats. He was fast lashing himself into one of his dreaded fits of blind fury. But Three-Eyes was oblivious of his presence. Her two outer eyes were tight shut and that strange, dreaded inner one was staring at *something*, something outside the limits of the cave, outside the framework of things as they are.

Deep in his throat the chief growled.

He raised the fine spear that was the symbol of his office and buried it deep in the old female's body. The inner eye shut and the two outer onces flickered open for the last time.

'I am spared the End –' she said.

Outside the little cavern the faithful Big-Ears was waiting.

'Three-Eyes is dead,' said his master. 'Take what you want, and give the rest to the People –'

For a little there was silence.

Then – 'I am glad you killed her,' said Wesel. 'She frightened me. I got inside her head – and I was lost!' Her voice had a hysterical edge. 'I was lost! It was mad, mad. *What Was* was a *place*, a *PLACE*, and *Now*, and *What Will Be*. And I saw the End.'

'What did you see?'

'A great light, far brighter than the Giants' lights Inside. And heat, stronger than the heat of the floors of the Far Outside caves and tunnels. And the People gasping and dying and the great light bursting into our world and eating them up –'

'But the Giants?'

'I did not see. I was lost. All I saw was the End.'

No-Fur was silent. His active, nimble mind was scurrying down the vistas opened up by the dead prophetess. Giant Killer *Giant Killer*. Even in his most grandiose dreams he had never seen himself thus. And what was that name? Shrick? He repeated it to himself – Shrick the Giant Killer. It had a fine swing to it. As for the rest, the End, if he could kill the Giants then surely he could stave off the doom that they would mete out to the People. Shrick, the Giant Killer –

'It is a name that I like better than No-Fur,' said Wesel.

'Shrick, Lord of the Outside. Shrick, Lord of the World, Shrick, the Giant Killer –'

'Yes,' he said, slowly. 'But the End –'

'You will go through that door when you come to it.'

The campaign against Tekka's People had opened.

Along the caves and tunnels poured the nightmare hordes of Shrick. The dim light but half revealed their misshapen bodies, limbs where no limbs should be, heads like something from a half forgotten bad dream.

All were armed. Every male and female carried a spear, and that in itself was a startling innovation in the wars of the People. For sharp metal, with which the weapons were tipped, was hard to come by. True, a staff of Barrier material could be sharpened, but it was a liability rather than an asset in a pitched battle. With the first thrust the point would break off, leaving the fighter with a weapon far inferior to his natural armory of teeth and claws.

Fire was new to the People – and it was Shrick who had brought them fire. For long periods he had spied upon the Giants in the Place-of-Little-Lights, had seen them bring from the pouches in their fur little, glittering devices from which when a projection was pressed, issued a tiny, naked light. And he had seen them bring this light to the end of strange, white sticks that they seemed to be sucking. And the end of the stick would glow, and there would be a cloud like the cloud that issued from the mouths of the People in some of the Far Outside caverns where it was very cold. But this cloud was fragrant, and seemed to be strangely soothing.

And one of the Giants had lost his little, hot light. He had put it to one of the white sticks, had made to return it to his pouch, and his hand had missed the opening. The Giant did not notice. He was doing something which took all his attention – and strain his eyes and his imagination as he might

Shrick could not see what it was. There were strange glittering machines through which he peered intently at the glittering Little Lights beyond their transparent Barrier. Or were they on the inside of the Barrier? Nobody had ever been able to decide. There was something alive that wasn't alive that clicked. There were sheets of fine, white skin on which the Giant was making black marks with a pointed stick.

But Shrick soon lost interest in these strange rites that he could never hope to comprehend. All his attention was focused on the glittering prize that was drifting ever so slowly towards him on the wings of some vagrant eddy.

When it seemed that it would surely fall right into the doorway where Shrick crouched waiting it swerved. And, much as he dreaded the pseudo life that hummed and clicked, Shrick came out. The Giant, busy with his sorcery, did not notice him. One swift leap carried him to the drifting trophy. And then he had it, tight clasped to his breast. It was bigger than he had thought, it having appeared so tiny only in relationship to its previous owner. But it wasn't too big to go through the door in the Barrier. In triumph Shrick bore it to his cave.

Many were the experiments that he, eager but fumbling, performed. For a while both he and Wesel nursed painful burns. Many were the experiments that he intended to perform in the future. But he had stumbled on one use for the hot light that was to be of paramount importance in his wars.

Aping the Giants, he had stuck a long splinter of Barrier material in his mouth. The end he had brought to the little light. There was, as he had half expected, a cloud. But it was neither fragrant nor soothing. Blinded and coughing, Wesel snatched at the glowing stick, beat out its strange life with her hands.

Then – 'It is hard,' she said. 'It is almost as hard as metal –'

And so Shrick became the first mass producer of armaments that his world had known. The first few sharpened staves he treated himself. The rest he left to Wesel and the faithful Big-Ears. He dare not trust his wonderful new power to any who were not among his intimates.

Shrick's other innovation was a direct violation of all the

rules of war. He had pressed the females into the fighting line. Those who were old and infirm, together with the old and infirm males, brought up the rear with bundles of the mass produced spears. The New People had been wondering for some little time why their chief had refused to let them slaughter those of their number who had outlived their usefulness. Now they knew.

The caves of the New People were deserted save for those few females with newborn.

And through the tunnels poured the hordes of Shrick.

There was little finesse in the campaign against Tekka's people. The outposts were slaughtered out of hand, but not before they had had time to warn the Tribe of the attack.

Tekka threw a body of picked spearmen into his van, confident that he, with better access to those parts of Inside where metal could be obtained, would be able to swamp the motley horde of the enemy with superior arms and numbers.

When Tekka saw, in the dim light, only a few betraying gleams of metal scattered among Shrick's massed spears he laughed.

'This No-Fur is mad,' he said. 'And I shall kill him with this.' He brandished his own weapon. 'His mother gave it to me many, many feedings ago.'

'Is Wesel – ?'

'Perhaps, my son. You shall eat her heart, I promise you.'

And then Shrick struck.

His screaming mob rushed along the wide tunnel. Confident the Tekkan spearmen waited, knowing that the enemy's weapons were good for only one thrust, and that almost certainly not lethal.

Tekka scowled as he estimated the numbers of the attackers. There couldn't be that many males among the New People. There couldn't – And then the wave struck.

In the twinkling of an eye the tunnel was tightly packed with struggling bodies. Here was no dignified, orderly, series of single combats such as had always, in the past, graced the wars of the People. And with growing terror Tekka realized that the enemy spears were standing up to the strain of battle at least as well as his own few metal-tipped weapons.

Slowly, but with ever mounting momentum, the attackers pressed on, gaining impetus from the many bodies that now lay behind them. Gasping for air in the effluvium of sweat and newly shed blood Tekka and the last of his guards were pressed back and ever back.

When one of the New People was disarmed he fell to the rear of his own front line. As though by magic a fresh fighter would appear to replace him.

Then – 'He's using females!' cried Trillo. 'He's –'

But Tekka did not answer. He was fighting for his life with a four-armed monster. Every hand held a spear – and every spear was bright with blood. For long heartbeats he parried the other's thrusts, then his nerve broke. Screaming, he turned his back on the enemy. It was the last thing he did.

And so the remnant of the fighting strength of the Tribe of Tekka was at last penned up against one wall of their Place-of-Meeting. Surrounding them was a solid hemisphere of the New People. Snarl was answered by snarl. Trillo and his scant half dozen guards knew that there was no surrender. All they could do was to sell their lives as dearly as possible.

And so they waited for the inevitable, gathering the last reserves of their strength in this lull of the battle, gasping the last sweet mouthfuls of air that they would ever taste. From beyond the wall of their assailants they could hear the cries and screams as the females and children, who had hidden in their caves, were hunted out and slaughtered. They were not to know that the magnanimous Shrick was sparing most of the females. They, he hoped, would produce for him more New People.

And then Shrick came, elbowing his way to the forefront of his forces. His smooth, naked body was unmarked, save by the old scars of his battle with Big-Tusk. And with him was Wesel, not a hair of her sleek fur out of place. And Big-Ears – but he, obviously, had been in the fight. With them came more fighters, fresh and eager.

'Finish them!' ordered Shrick.

'Wait!' Wesel's voice was imperative. 'I want Trillo.'

Him she pointed out to the picked fighters, who raised their spears – weapons curiously slender and light, too fragile for hand-to-hand combat. A faint hope stirred in the breasts of the last defenders.

'Now!'

Trillo and his guards braced themselves to meet the last rush. It never came. Instead, thrown with unerring aim, came those sharp, flimsy spears, pinning them horribly against the gray, spongy wall of the Place-of-Meeting.

Spared in this final slaughter, Trillo looked about him with wide, fear-crazed eyes. He started to scream, then launched himself at the laughing Wesel. But she slipped back through the packed masses of the New People. Blind to all else but that hateful figure, Trillo tried to follow. And the New People crowded about him, binding his arms and legs with their strong cords, snatching his spear from him before its blade drank blood.

Then again the captive saw she who had been his mate.

Shamelessly, she was caressing Shrick.

'My Hairless One,' she said. 'I was once mated to *this*. You shall have his fur to cover your smooth body.' And then – 'Big-Ears! You know what to do!'

Grinning, Big-Ears found the sharp blade of a spear that had become detached from its haft. Grinning, he went to work. Trillo started to whimper, then to scream. Shrick felt a little sick.

'Stop!' he said. 'He is not dead. You must –'

'What does it matter?' Wesel's eyes were avid, and her little, pink tongue came out to lick her thin lips. Big-Ears had hesitated in his work but, at her sign, continued.

'What does it matter?' she said again.

As had fared the Tribe of Tekka so fared the Tribe of Sterret, and a hand or more of smaller communities owing a loose allegiance to these two.

But it was in his war with Sterret that Shrick almost met disaster. To the cunning oldster had come survivors from the

36

massacre of Tekka's army. Most of these had been slaughtered out of hand by the frontier guards, but one or two had succeeded in convincing their captors that they bore tidings of great importance.

Sterret heard them out.

He ordered that they be fed and treated as his own people, for he knew that he would need every ounce of fighting strength that he could muster.

Long and deeply he pondered upon their words, and then sent foray after foray of his young males to the Place-of-Life-That-is-Not-Life. Careless he was of detection by the Giants. They might or might not act against him – but he had long been convinced that, for all their size, they were comparatively stupid and harmless. Certainly, at this juncture, they were not such a menace as Shrick, already self-styled Lord of the Outside.

And so his store of sharp fragments of metal grew, whilst his armorers worked without cessation binding these to hafts of Barrier stuff. And he, too, could innovate. Some of the fragments were useless as spearheads, being blunt, rough, and irregular. But, bound like a spearhead to a shaft, they could deliver a crushing blow. Of this Sterret was sure after a few experiments on old and unwanted members of his Tribe.

Most important, perhaps, his mind, rich in experience but not without a certain youthful zest, busied itself with problems of strategy. In the main tunnel from what had been Tekka's country his females hacked and tore at the spongy wall, the material being packed tightly and solidly into another small tunnel that was but rarely used.

At last his scouts brought the word that Shrick's forces were on the move. Careless in the crushing weight of his military power, Shrick disdained anything but a direct frontal attack. Perhaps he should have been warned by the fact that all orifices admitting light from the Inside had been closed, that the main tunnel along which he was advancing was in total darkness.

This, however, hampered him but little. The body of picked spearmen opposing him fought in the conventional way, and these, leaving their dead and wounded, were forced slowly but surely back. Each side relied upon smell, and hearing, and a certain perception possessed by most, if not all, of the People. At such close quarters these were ample.

Shrick himself was not in the van – that honor was reserved for Big-Ears, his fighting general. Had the decision rested with him alone he would have been in the forefront of the battle – but Wesel averred that the leader was of far greater importance than a mere spear bearer, should be shielded from needless risk. Not altogether unwillingly, Shrick acquiesced.

Surrounded by his guard, with Wesel at his side, the leader followed the noise of the fighting. He was rather surprised at the reports coming back to him concerning the apparent numbers of the enemy, but assumed that this was a mere delaying action and that Sterret would make his last stand in the Place-of-Meeting. It never occurred to him in his arrogance that others could innovate.

Abruptly, Wesel clutched his arm.

'Shrick! Danger – from the side!'

'From the side? But –'

There was a shrill cry, and a huge section of the tunnel wall fell inwards. The spongy stuff was in thin sheets, and drifted among the guard, hampering their every movement. Then, led by Sterret in person, the defenders came out. Like mountaineers they were roped together, for in this battle in the darkness their best hope lay in keeping in one, compact body. Separated, they would fall easy prey to the superior numbers of the hordes of Shrick.

With spear and mace they lay about them lustily. The first heartbeat of the engagement would have seen the end of Shrick, and it was only the uncured hide of Trillo, stiff and stinking, that saved his life. Even so, the blade of Sterret penetrated the crude armor, and, sorely wounded, Shrick reeled out of the battle.

Ahead, Big-Ears was no longer having things all his own way. Reinforcements had poured along the tunnel and he dare not return to the succor of his chief. And Sterret's maces were having their effect. Stabbing and slashing the People could understand – but a crushing blow was, to them, something infinitely horrible.

It was Wesel who saved the day. With her she had brought the little, hot light. It had been her intention to try its effect on such few prisoners as might be taken in this campaign – she was too shrewd to experiment on any of the New People, even those who had incurred the displeasure of herself or her mate.

Scarce knowing what she did she pressed the stud.

With dazzling suddenness the scene of carnage swam into full view. From all sides came cries of fear.

'Back!' cried Wesel. 'Back! Clear a space!'

In two directions the New People retreated.

Blinking but dogged, Sterret's phalanx tried to follow, tried to turn what was a more or less orderly withdrawal into a rout. But the cords that had, at first, served them so well now proved their undoing. Some tried to pursue those making for the Place-of-Meeting, others those of the New People retiring to their own territory. Snarling viciously, blood streaming from a dozen minor wounds, Sterret at last cuffed and bullied his forces into a semblance of order. He attempted to lead a charge to where Wesel, the little, hot light still in her hand, was retreating among her personal, amazon guards.

But again the cunning – too cunning – ropes defeated his purpose. Not a few corpses were there to hamper fast movement, and almost none of his fighters had the intelligence to cut them free.

And the spear throwers of Shrick came to the fore, and, one by one, the people of Sterret were pinned by the slim deadly shafts to the tunnel walls. Not all were killed outright, a few unfortunates squirmed and whimpered, plucking at the spears with ineffectual hands.

Among these was Sterret.

Shrick came forward, spear in hand, to administer the *coup de grace*. The old chief stared wildly, then – 'Weena's hairless one!' he cried.

Ironically it was his own spear – the weapon that, in turn,

39

had belonged to Weena and to Tekka – that slit his throat.

Now that he was Lord of the Outside Shrick had time in which to think and to dream. More and more his mind harked back to Three-Eyes and her prophesy. It never occurred to him to doubt that he was to be the Giant Killer – although the vision of the End he dismissed from his mind as the vaporings of a half-crazed old female.

And so he sent his spies to the Inside to watch the Giants in their mysterious comings and goings, tried hard to find some pattern for their incomprehensible behavior. He himself often accompanied these spies – and it was with avid greed that he saw the vast wealth of beautiful, shining things to which the Giants were heir. More than anything he desired another little hot light, for his own had ceased to function, and all the clumsy ignorant tinkerings of himself and Wesel could not produce more than a feeble, almost heatless spark from its baffling intricacies.

It seemed, too, that the Giants were now aware of the swarming, fecund life surrounding them. Certain it was that their snares increased in number and ingenuity. And the food-that-kills appeared in new and terrifying guise. Not only did those who had eaten of it die, but their mates and – indeed all who had come into contact with them.

It smacked of sorcery, but Shrick had learned to associate cause and effect. He made the afflicted ones carry those already dead into a small tunnel. One or two of them rebelled – but the spear throwers surrounded them, their slim, deadly weapons at the ready. And those who attempted to break through the cordon of guards were run through repeatedly before ever they laid their defiling hands on any of the un-afflicted People.

Big-Ears was among the sufferers. He made no attempt to quarrel with his fate. Before he entered the yawning tunnel that was to be his tomb he turned and looked at his chief. Shrick made to call him to his side – even though he knew that his friend's life could not be saved, and that by associating with him he would almost certainly lose his own.

40

But Wesel was at his side.

She motioned to the spear throwers, and a full two hands of darts transfixed the ailing Big-Ears.

'It was kinder this way,' she lied.

But, somehow, the last look that his most loyal supporter had given him reminded him of No-Tail. With a heavy heart he ordered his people to seal the tunnel. Great strips of the spongy stuff were brought and stuffed into the entrance. The cries of those inside grew fainter and ever fainter. Then there was silence. Shrick ordered guards posted at all points where, conceivably, the doomed prisoners might break out. He returned to his own cave. Wesel, when one without her gift would have intruded, let him go in his loneliness. Soon he would want her again.

It had long been Wesel's belief that, given the opportunity, she could get inside the minds of the Giants just as she could those of the People. And if she could – who knew what prizes might be hers? Shrick, still inaccessible and grieving for his friend, she missed more than she cared to admit. The last of the prisoners from the last campaign had been killed, ingeniously, many feedings ago. Though she had no way of measuring time it hung heavily on her hands.

And so, accompanied by two of her personal attendants, she roamed those corridors and tunnels running just inside the Barrier. Through spyhole after spyhole she peered, gazing in wonderment that long use could not stale at the rich and varied life of the Inside.

At last she found that for which she was searching – a Giant, alone and sleeping. Experience among the People had taught her that from a sleeping mind she could read the most secret thoughts.

For a heartbeat she hesitated. Then – 'Four-Arms, Little-Head, wait here for me. Wait and watch.'

Little-Head grunted an affirmative, but Four-Arms was dubious. 'Lady Wesel,' she said, 'what if the Giant should wake? What – ?'

'What if you should return to the Lord of the Outside without me? Then he would, without doubt, have your hides. The one he is wearing now is old, and the fur is coming out. But do as I say.'

There was a door in the Barrier here, a door but rarely used. This was opened, and Wesel slipped through. With the ease that all the People were acquiring with their more frequent ventures to the Inside she floated up to the sleeping Giant. Bonds held him in a sort of framework, and Wesel wondered if, for some offense, he had been made prisoner by his own kind. She would soon know.

And then a glittering object caught her eye. It was one of the little, hot lights, its polished metal case seeming to Wesel's covetous eyes the most beautiful thing in the world. Swiftly she made her decision. She could take the shining prize now, deliver it to her two attendants, and then return to carry out her original intentions.

In her eagerness she did not see that it was suspended in the middle of an interlacing of slender metal bars – or she did not care. And as her hands grabbed the bait something not far away began a shrill, not unmusical metalling beating. The Giant stirred and awoke. What Wesel had taken for bonds fell away from his body. In blind panic she turned to flee back to her own world. But, somehow, more of the metal bars had fallen into place and she was a prisoner.

She started to scream.

Surprisingly, Four-Arms and Little-Head came to her aid. It would be nice to be able to place on record that they were actuated by devotion to their mistress – but Four-Arms knew that her life was forfeit. And she had seen those who displeased either Shrick or Wesel flayed alive. Little-Head blindly followed the other's leadership. Hers not to reason why –

Slashing with their spears they assailed the Giant. He laughed – or so Wesel interpreted the deep, rumbling sound that came from his throat. Four-Arms he seized first. With one hand he grasped her body, with the other her head. He twisted. And that was the end of Four-Arms.

Anybody else but Little-Head would have turned and fled.

But her dim mind refused to register that which she had seen. Perhaps a full feeding or so after the event the horror of it all would have stunned her with its impact – perhaps not. Be that as it may, she continued her attack. Blindly, instinctively, she went for the Giant's throat. Wesel sensed that he was badly frightened. But after a short struggle one of his hands caught the frenzied, squealing Little-Head. Violently, he flung her from him. She heard the thud as her attendant's body struck something hard and unyielding. And the impressions that her mind had been receiving from that of the other abruptly ceased.

Even in her panic and fear she noticed that the Giant had not come out of the unequal combat entirely unscathed. One of his hands had been scratched, and was bleeding freely. And there were deep scratches on the hideous, repulsively naked face. The Giants, then, were vulnerable. There might have been some grain of truth after all in Three-Eyes' insane babbling.

And then Wesel forgot her unavailing struggle against the bars of her cage. With sick horror she watched what the Giant was doing. He had taken the limp body of Four-Arms, had secured it to a flat surface. From somewhere he had produced an array of glittering instruments. One of these he took, and drew it down the body from throat to crotch. On either side of the keen blade the skin fell away, leaving the flesh exposed.

And the worst part of it was that it was not being done in hate or anger, neither was the unfortunate Four-Arms being divided up that she might be eaten. There was an impersonal quality about the whole business that sickened Wesel – for, by this time, she had gained a certain limited access to the mind of the other.

The Giant paused in his work. Another of his kind had come, and for many heartbeats the two talked together. They examined the mutilated carcass of Four-Arms, the crushed body of Little-Head. Together, they peered into the cage where Wesel snarled impotently.

But, in spite of her hysterical fear, part of her mind was deadly cold, was receiving and storing impressions that threw the uninhibited, animal part of her into still greater panic.

Whilst the Giants talked the impressions were clear – and whilst their great, ungainly heads hung over her cage, scant handsbreadths away, they were almost overpowering in their strength. She knew who she and the People were, what their world was. She had not the ability to put it into words – but she *knew*. And she saw the doom that the Giants were preparing for the People.

With a few parting words to his fellow the second Giant left. The first one resumed his work of dismembering Four-Arms. At last he was finished. What was left of the body was put into transparent containers.

The Giant picked up Little-Head. For many heartbeats he examined her, turning her over and over in his great hands. Wesel thought that he would bind the body to the flat surface, do with it as he had done with that of Four-Arms. But, at last he put the body to one side. Over his hands he pulled something that looked like a thick, additional skin. Suddenly, the metal bars at one end of the cage fell away, and one of those enormous hands came groping for Wesel.

After the death of Big-Ears, Shrick slept a little. It was the only way in which he could be rid of the sense of loss, of the feeling that he had betrayed his most loyal follower. His dreams were troubled, haunted by ghosts from his past. Big-Ears was in them, and Big-Tusk, and a stranger female with whom he felt a sense of oneness, whom he knew to be Weena, his mother.

And then all these phantasms were gone, leaving only the image of Wesel. It wasn't the Wesel he had always known, cool, self-assured, ambitious. This was a terrified Wesel – Wesel descending into a black abyss of pain and torture even worse than that which she had, so often, meted out to others. And she wanted him.

Shrick awoke, frightened by his dreams. But he knew that ghosts had never hurt anybody, could not hurt him, Lord of the Outside. He shook himself, whimpering a little and then tried to compose himself for further sleep.

But the image of Wesel persisted. At last Shrick abandoned his attempts to seek oblivion and, rubbing his eyes, emerged from his cave.

In the dim, half-light of the Place-of-Meeting little knots of the People hung about, talking in low voices. Shrick called to the guards. There was a sullen silence. He called again. At last one answered.

'Where is Wesel?'

'I do not know . . . lord.' The last word came out grudgingly.

Then one of the others volunteered the information that she had been seen, in company with Four-Arms and Little-Head, proceeding along the tunnels that led to that part of the Outside in the way of the Place-of-Green-Growing-Things.

Shrick hesitated.

He rarely ventured abroad without his personal guards, but then, Big-Ears was always one of them. And Big-Ears was gone.

He looked around him, decided that he could trust none of those at present in the Place-of-Meeting. The People had been shocked and horrified by his necessary actions in the case of those who had eaten of the food-that-kills and regarded him, he knew, as a monster even worse than the Giants. Their memories were short – but until they forgot he would have to walk with caution.

'Wesel is my mate. I will go alone,' he said.

At his words he sensed a change of mood, was tempted to demand an escort. But the instinct that – as much as any mental superiority – maintained him in authority warned him against throwing away his advantage.

'I go alone,' he said.

One Short-Tail, bolder than his fellows, spoke up.

'And if you do not return, Lord of the Outside? Who is to be – ?'

'I shall return,' said Shrick firmly, his voice displaying a confidence he did not feel.

In the more populous regions the distinctive scent of Wesel was overhid by that of many others. In tunnels but rarely frequented it was strong and compelling – but now he had no need to use his olfactory powers. For the terrified little voice in his

45

brain – from outside his brain – was saying *hurry, HURRY* – and some power beyond his ken was guiding him unerringly to where his mate was in such desperate need of him.

From the door in the Barrier through which Wesel had entered the Inside – it had been left open – streamed a shaft of light. And now Shrick's natural caution reasserted itself. The voice inside his brain was no less urgent, but the instinct of self-preservation was strong. Almost timorously, he peered through the doorway.

He smelled death. At first he feared that he was too late, then identified the personal odors of Four-Arms and Little-Head. That of Wesel was there too – intermingled with the acrid scent of terror and agony. But she was still alive.

Caution forgotten, he launched himself from the doorway with all the power of his leg muscles. And he found Wesel, stretched supine on a flat surface that was slippery with blood. Most of it was Four-Arms', but some of it was hers.

'Shrick!' she screamed. 'The Giant!'

He looked away from his mate and saw hanging over him, pale and enormous, the face of the Giant. He screamed, but there was more of fury than terror in the sound. He saw, not far from where he clung to Wesel, a huge blade of shining metal. He could see that its edge was keen. The handle had been fashioned for a hand far larger than his, nevertheless he was just able to grasp it. It seemed to be secured. Feet braced against Wesel's body for purchase, he tugged desperately.

Just as the Giant's hand, fingers outstretched to seize him, came down the blade pulled free. As Shrick's legs suddenly and involuntarily straightened he was propelled away from Wesel. The Giant grabbed at the flying form, and howled in agony as Shrick swept the blade around and lopped off a finger.

He heard Wesel's voice: 'You are the Giant Killer!'

Now he was level with the Giant's head. He swerved, and with his feet caught a fold of the artificial skin covering the huge body. And he hung there, swinging his weapon with both hands, cutting and slashing. Great hands swung wildly and he was bruised and buffeted. But not once did they succeed in

46

finding a grip. Then there was a great and horrid spurting of blood and a wild threshing of mighty limbs. This ceased, but it was only the voice of Wesel that called him from the fury of his slaughter lust.

So he found her again, still stretched out for sacrifice to the Giants' dark gods, still bound to that surface that was wet with her blood and that of her attendant. But she smiled up at him, and in her eyes was respect that bordered on awe.

'Are you hurt?' he demanded, a keen edge of anxiety to his voice.

'Only a little. But Four-Arms was cut in pieces . . . I should have been had you not come. And,' her voice was a hymn of praise, 'you killed the Giant!'

'It was foretold. Besides,' for once he was honest, 'it could not have been done without the Giant's weapon.'

With its edge he was cutting Wesel's bonds. Slowly she floated away from the place of sacrifice. Then: 'I can't move my legs!' Her voice was terror-stricken. 'I can't move!'

Shrick guessed what was wrong. He knew a little of anatomy – his knowledge was that of the warrior who may be obliged to immobilize his enemy prior to his slaughter – and he could see that the Giant's keen blade had wrought this damage. Fury boiled up in him against these cruel, monstrous beings. And there was more than fury. There was the feeling, rare among his people, of overwheling pity for his crippled mate.

'The blade . . . it is very sharp . . . I shall feel nothing.'

But Shrick could not bring himself to do it.

Now they were floating up against the huge bulk of the dead Giant. With one hand he grasped Wesel's shoulder – the other still clutched his fine, new weapon – and kicked off against the gigantic carcass. Then he was pushing Wesel through the doorway in the Barrier, and sensed her relief as she found herself once more in familiar territory. He followed her, then carefully shut and barred the door.

For a few heartbeats Wesel busied herself smoothing her bedraggled fur. He couldn't help noticing that she dare not let her hands stray to the lower part of her body where were the

47

wounds, small but deadly, that had robbed her of the power of her limbs. Dimly, he felt that something might be done for one so injured, but knew that it was beyond his powers. And fury – not helpless now – against the Giants returned again, threatening to choke him with its intensity.

'Shrick!' Wesel's voice was grave. 'We must return at once to the People. We must warn the People. The Giants are making a sorcery to bring the End.'

'The great, hot light?'

'No. But wait! First I must tell you of what I learned. otherwise, you would not believe. I have learned what we are, what the world is. And it is strange and wonderful beyond all our beliefs.

'What is Outside?' She did not wait for his answer, read it in his mind before his lips could frame the words. 'The world is but a bubble of emptiness in the midst of a vast piece of metal, greater than the mind can imagine. But it is not so! Outside the metal that lies outside the Outside there is nothing. *Nothing!* There is no air.'

'But there must be air, at least.'

'No, I tell you. There is *nothing*.

'And the world – how can I find words? Their name for the world is – *ship*, and it seems to mean something big going from one place to another place. And all of us – Giants and People – are inside the ship. The Giants made the ship.'

'Then it is not alive?'

'I cannot say. *They* seem to think that it is a female. It must have some kind of life that is not life. And it is going from one world to another world.'

'And these other worlds?'

'I caught glimpses of them. They are dreadful, dreadful. *We* find the open spaces of the Inside frightening – but these other worlds are *all* open space except for one side.'

'But what are we?' In spite of himself, Shrick at least half believed Wesel's fantastic story. Perhaps she possessed, to some slight degree, the power of projecting her own thoughts into the mind of another with whom she was intimate. 'What are we?'

48

She was silent for the space of many heartbeats. Th n: *'Their* name for us is – *mutants.* The picture was . . . not clear at all. It means that we – the People – have changed. And yet their picture of the People before the change was like the Different Ones before we slew them all.

'Long and long ago – many hands of feedings – the first People, our parents' parents' parents, came into the world. They came from that greater world – the world of dreadful, open spaces. They came with the food in the great Cave-of-Food – and that is being carried to another world.

'Now, in the horrid, empty space outside the Outside there is – light that is not light. And this light – changes persons. No, not the grown person or the child, but the child before the birth. Like the dead and gone chiefs of the People, the Giants fear change in themselves. So they have kept the light that is not light from the Inside.

'And this is how. Between the Barrier and the Far Outside they filled the space with the stuff in which we have made our caves and tunnels. The first People left the great Cave-of-Food, they tunneled through the Barrier. It was their nature. And some of them mated in the Far Outside caves. Their children were – *Different.'*

'That is true,' said Shrick slowly. 'It has always been thought that children born in the Far Outside were never like their parents, and that those born close to the Barrier were –'

'Yes.

'Now, the Giants always knew that the People were here, but they did not fear them. They did not know our numbers, and they regarded us as beings much lower than themselves. They were content to keep us down with their traps and the food-that-kills. Somehow, they found that we had changed. Like the dead chiefs they feared us then – and like the dead chiefs they will try to kill us all before we conquer them.'

'And the End ?'

'Yes, the End.' She was silent again, her big eyes looking past Shrick at something infinitely terrible. 'Yes,' she said again, 'the End. *They* will make it, and *They* will escape it. *They* will put on artificial skins that will cover *Their* whole

49

bodies, even *Their* heads, and *They* will open huge doors in the . . . skin of the ship, and all the air will rush out into the terrible empty space outside the Outside. And all the People will die.'

'I must go,' said Shrick. 'I must kill the Giants before this comes to pass.'

'No! There was one hand of Giants – now that you have killed Fat-Belly there are four of them left. And they know, now, that they can be killed. They will be watching for you.

'Do you remember when we buried the People with the sickness? That is what we must do to all the People. And then when the Giants fill the world with air again from their store we can come out.'

Shrick was silent awhile. He had to admit that she was right. One unsuspecting Giant had fallen to his blade – but four of them, aroused, angry and watchful, he could not handle. In any case there was no way of knowing when the Giants would let the air from the world. The People must be warned – and fast.

Together, in the Place-of-Meeting, Shrick and Wesel faced the People. They had told their stories, only to be met with blank incredulity. True, there were some who, seeing the fine, shining blade that Shrick had brought from the Inside, were inclined to believe. But they were shouted down by the majority. It was when he tried to get them to immure themselves against the End that he met with serious opposition. The fact that he had so treated those suffering from the sickness still bulked big in the mob memory.

It was Short-Tail who precipitated the crisis.

'He wants the world to himself!' he shouted. 'He has killed Big-Tusk and No-Tail, he has killed all the Different Ones, and Big-Ears he slew because he would have been chief. He and his ugly, barren mate want the world to themselves!'

Shrick tried to argue, but Big-Ears' following shouted him down. He squealed with rage and raising his blade with both hands, rushed upon the rebel. Short-Tail scurried back out of reach. Shrick found himself alone in a suddenly cleared space.

From somewhere a long way off he heard Wesel screaming his name. Dazedly, he shook his head, and then the red mist cleared from in front of his eyes.

All around him were the spear throwers, their slender weapons poised. He had trained them himself, had brought their specialized art of war into being. And now –

'Shrick!' Wesel was saying, 'don't fight! They will kill you, and I shall be alone. I shall have the world to myself. Let them do as they will with us, and *we* shall live through the End.'

At her words a tittering laugh rippled through the mob.

'*They* will live through the End! They will die as Big-Ears and his friends died!'

'I want your blade,' said Short-Tail.

'Give it to him,' cried Wesel. 'You will get it back after the End!'

Shrick hesitated. The other made a sign. One of the throwing spears buried itself in the fleshy part of his arm. Had it not been for Wesel's voice, pleading, insistent, he would have charged his tormenters and met his end in less than a single heartbeat. Reluctantly, he released his hold upon the weapon. Slowly – as though loath to leave its true owner – it floated away from him. And then the People were all around him, almost suffocating him with the pressure of their bodies.

The cave into which Shrick and Wesel were forced was their own dwelling place. They were in pitiable state when the mob retreated to the entrance – Wesel's wounds had reopened and Shrick's arm was bleeding freely. Somebody had wrenched out the spear – but the head had broken off.

Outside, Short-Tail was laying about him with the keen blade he had taken from his chief. Under its strokes great masses of the spongy stuff of the Outside were coming free, and many willing hands were stuffing this tight into the cave entrance.

'We will let you out after the End!' called somebody. There was a hoot of derision. Then: 'I wonder which will eat the other first?'

'Never mind,' said Wesel softly. 'We shall laugh last.'

'Perhaps. But . . . the People. *My* People. And you are barren. The Giants have won –'

Wesel was silent. Then he heard her voice again. She was whimpering to herself in the darkness. Shrick could guess her thoughts. All their grandiose dreams of world dominion had come to this – a tiny, cramped space in which there was barely room for either of them to stir a finger.

And now they could no longer hear the voices of the People outside their prison. Shrick wondered if the Giants had already struck, then reassured himself with the memory of how the voices of those suffering from the sickness had grown fainter and fainter and then, at the finish, ceased altogether. And he wondered how he and Wesel would know when the End had come, and how they would know when it was safe to dig themselves out. It would be a long, slow task with only their teeth and claws with which to work.

But he had a tool.

The fingers of the hand of his uninjured arm went to the spearhead still buried in the other. He knew that by far the best way of extracting it would be one, quick pull – but he couldn't bring himself to do it. Slowly, painfully, he worked away at the sharp fragment of metal.

'Let me do it for you.'

'No.' His voice was rough. 'Besides, there is no haste.'

Slowly, patiently, he worried at the wound. He was groaning a little, although he was not conscious of doing so. And then, suddenly Wesel screamed. The sound was so unexpected, so dreadful in that confined space, that Shrick started violently. His hand jerked away from his upper arm, bringing with it the spearhead.

His first thought was that Wesel, telepath as she was, had chosen this way to help him. But he felt no gratitude, only a dull resentment.

'What did you do that for?' he demanded angrily.

She didn't answer his question. She was oblivious of his presence.

'The People . . .' she whispered, 'the People . . . I can feel their thoughts . . . I can feel what they are feeling. And they

52

are gasping for air . . . they are gasping and dying . . . and the cave of Long-Fur the spearmaker . . . but they are dying, and the blood is coming out of their mouths and noses and ears . . . I can't bear it . . . I can't –'

And then a terrifying thing happened. The sides of the cave pressed in upon them. Throughout the world, throughout the ship, the air cells in the spongy insulation were expanding as the air pressure dropped to zero. It was this alone that saved Shrick and Wesel, although they never knew it. The rough plug sealing their cave that, otherwise, would have blown out swelled to meet the expanding walls of the entrance, making a near perfect air-tight joint.

But the prisoners were in no state to appreciate this, even had they been in possession of the necessary knowledge. Panic seized them both. Claustrophobia was unknown among the People – but walls that closed upon them were outside their experience.

Perhaps Wesel was the more level-headed of the pair. It was she who tried to restrain her mate as he clawed and bit savagely, madly, at the distended, bulging walls. He no longer knew what lay outside the cave, had he known it would have made no difference. His one desire was to get out.

At first he made little headway, then he bethought himself of the little blade still grasped in his hand. With it he attacked the pulpy mass. The walls of the cells were stretched thin, almost to bursting, and under his onslaught they put up no more resistance than so many soap bubbles. A space was cleared, and Shrick was able to work with even greater vigor.

'Stop! Stop, I tell you! There is only the choking death outside the cave. And you will kill us both!'

But Shrick paid no heed, went on stabbing and hacking. It was only slowly, now, that he was able to enlarge upon the original impression he had made. As the swollen surfaces burst and withered beneath his blade, so they bulged and bellied in fresh places.

'Stop!' cried Wesel again.

With her arms, her useless legs trailing behind her, she pulled herself towards her mate. And she grappled with him,

53

desperation lending her strength. So for many heartbeats they fought – silent, savage, forgetful of all that each owed to the other. And yet, perhaps, Wesel never quite forgot. For all her blind, frantic will to survive her telepathic powers were at no time entirely in abeyance. In spite of herself she, as always, shared the other's mind. And this psychological factor gave her an advantage that offset the paralysis of the lower half of her body – and at the same time inhibited her from pressing that advantage home to its logical conclusion.

But it did not save her when her fingers, inadvertently, dug into the wound in Shrick's arm. His earsplitting scream was compounded of pain and fury, and he drew upon reserves of strength that the other never even guessed that he possessed. And the hand gripping the blade came round with irresistible force.

For Wesel there was a heartbeat of pain, of sorrow for herself and Shrick, of blind anger against the Giants who, indirectly, had brought this thing to pass.

And then the beating of her heart was stilled forever.

With the death of Wesel Shrick's frenzy left him.

There, in the darkness, he ran his sensitive fingers over the lifeless form, hopelessly hoping for the faintest sign of life. He called her name, he shook her roughly. But at last the knowledge that she was dead crept into his brain – and stayed there. In his short life he had known many times this sense of loss, but never with such poignancy.

And worst of all was the knowledge that *he* had killed her.

He tried to shift the burden of blame. He told himself that she would have died, in any case, of the wounds received at the hands of the Giants. He tried to convince himself that, wounds or no wounds, the Giants were directly responsible for her death. And he knew that he was Wesel's murderer, just as he knew that all that remained for him in life was to bring the slayers of his people to a reckoning.

This made him cautious.

For many heartbeats he lay there in the thick darkness, not daring to renew his assault on the walls of his prison. He told

54

himself that, somehow, he would know when the Giants let the air back into the world. How he would know he could not say, but the conviction persisted.

And when at last, with returning pressure, the insulation resumed its normal consistency, Shrick took this as a sign that it was safe for him to get out. He started to hack at the spongy material, then stopped. He went back to the body of Wesel. Just once he whispered her name, and ran his hands over the stiff, silent form in a last caress.

He did not return.

And when, at last, the dim light of the Place-of-Meeting broke through she was buried deep in the debris that he had thrown behind him as he worked.

The air tasted good after the many times breathed atmosphere of the cave. For a few heartbeats Shrick was dizzy with the abrupt increase of pressure, for much of the air in his prison had escaped before the plug expanded to seal the entrance. It is probable that had it not been for the air liberated from the burst cells of the insulation he would long since have asphyxiated.

But this he was not to know – and if he had known it would not have worried him overmuch. He was alive, and Wesel and all the People were dead. When the mist cleared from in front of his eyes he could see them, their bodies twisted in the tortuous attitudes of their last agony, mute evidence of the awful powers of the Giants.

And now that he saw them he did not feel the overwhelming sorrow that he knew he should have done. He felt instead a kind of anger. By their refusal to heed his warning they had robbed him of his kingdom. None now could dispute his mastery of the Outside – but with no subjects, willing or unwilling, the vast territory under his sway was worthless.

With Wesel alive it would have been different.

What was it that she had said – ? ... *and the cave of Long-Fur the spear maker* ...

He could hear her voice as she said it ... *and the cave of Long-Fur the spear maker.*

Perhaps – But there was only one way to make sure.

He found the cave, saw that its entrance had been walled up. He felt a wild upsurge of hope. Frantically, with tooth and claw, he tore at the insulation. The fine blade that he had won from the Inside gleamed dully not a dozen handsbreadths from where he was working, but such was his blind, unreasoning haste that he ignored the tool that would have made his task immeasurably shorter. At last the entrance was cleared. A feeble cry greeted the influx of air and light. For a while Shrick could not see who was within, and then could have screamed in his disappointment.

For here were no tough fighting males, no sturdy, fertile females, but two hands or so of weakly squirming infants. Their mothers must have realized, barely in time, that he and Wesel had been right, that there was only one way to ward off the choking death. Themselves they had not been able to save.

But they will grow up, Shrick told himself. *It won't be long before they are able to carry a spear for the Lord of the Outside, before the females are able to bear his children.*

Conquering his repugnance, he dragged them out. There was a hand of female infants, all living, and a hand of males. Three of these were dead. But here, he knew, was the nucleus of the army with which he would re-establish his rule over the world, Inside as well as Outside.

But first, they had to be fed.

He saw, now, his fine blade, and seizing it he began to cut up the three lifeless male children. The scent of their blood made him realize that he was hungry. But it was not until the children, now quieted, were all munching happily that he cut a portion for himself.

When he had finished it he felt much better.

It was some time before Shrick resumed his visits to the Inside. He had the pitiful remnant of his people to nurse to maturity and, besides, there was no need to make raids upon the Giants' stocks of food. They themselves had provided him with sustenance beyond his powers of reckoning. He knew, too, that it would be unwise to let his enemies know that there had been any survivors from the cataclysm that they had launched.

56

The fact that he had survived the choking death did not mean that it was the only weapon that the Giants had at their disposal.

But as time went on he felt an intense longing to watch once more the strange life beyond the Barrier. Now that he had killed a Giant he felt a strange sense of kinship with the monstrous beings. He thought of the Thin-One, Loud-Voice, Bare-Head and the Little Giant almost as old friends. At times he even caught himself regretting that he must kill them all. But he knew that in this lay the only hope for the survival of himself and his people.

And then, at last, he was satisfied that he could leave the children to fend for themselves. Even should he fail to return from the Inside they would manage. No-Toes, the eldest of the female children, had already proved to be a capable nurse.

And so he roamed once more the maze of caves and tunnels just outside the Barrier. Through his doorways and peepholes he spied upon the bright, fascinating life of the Inner World. From the Cave-of-Thunders – though how it had come by its name none of the People had ever known – to the Place-of-Little-Lights he ranged. Many feedings passed, but he was not obliged to return to his own food store. For the corpses of the People were everywhere. True, they were beginning to stink a little, but like all his race Shrick was never a fastidious eater.

And he watched the Giants going about the strange, ordered routine of their lives. Often he was tempted to show himself, to shout defiance. But this action had to remain in the realm of wishfulfillment dreams – he knew full well that it would bring sure and speedy calamity.

And then, at last, came the opportunity for which he had been waiting. He had been in the Place-of-Little-Lights, watching the Little Giant going about his mysterious absorbing business. He had wished that he could understand its purport, that he could ask the Little Giant in his own tongue what it was that he was doing. For, since the death of Wesel, there had been none with whom a communion of mind was possible. He sighed, so loudly that the Giant must have heard.

He started uneasily and looked up from his work. Hastily

Shrick withdrew into his tunnel. For many heartbeats he remained there, occasionally peeping out. But the other was still alert, must have known in some way that he was not alone. And so, eventually, Shrick had retired rather than risk incurring the potent wrath of the Giants once more.

His random retreat brought him to a doorway but rarely used. On the other side of it was a huge cavern in which there was nothing of real interest or value. In it, as a rule, at least one of the Giants would be sleeping, and others would be engaged in one of their incomprehensible pastimes.

This time there was no deep rumble of conversation, no movement whatsoever. Shrick's keen ears could distinguish the breathing of three different sleepers. The Thin-One was there, his respiration, like himself, had a meager quality. Loud-Voice was loud even in sleep. And Bare-Head, the chief of the Giants, breathed with a quiet authority.

And the Little Giant who, alone of all his people, was alert and awake was in the Place-of-Little-Lights.

Shrick knew that it was now or never. Any attempt to deal with the Giants singly must surely bring the great, hot light foretold by Three-Eyes. Now, with any luck at all, he could deal with the three sleepers and then lay in wait for the Little Giant. Unsuspecting, unprepared, he could be dealt with as easily as had Fat-Belly.

And yet – he did not want to do it.

It wasn't fear; it was that indefinable sense of kinship, the knowledge that, in spite of gross physical disparities, the Giants and the People were as one. For the history of Man, although Shrick was not to know this, is but the history of the fire-making, tool-using animal.

Then he forced himself to remember Wesel, and Big-Ears, and the mass slaughter of almost all his race. He remembered Three-Eyes' words – *but this I can tell you, the People are doomed. Nothing you or they can do will save them. But you will kill those who will kill us, and that is good.*

But you will kill those who will like us –

But if I kill all the Giants before they kill us, he thought, then the world, all the world, will belong to the People . . .

And still he hung back.

It was not until the Thin-One, who must have been in the throes of a bad dream, murmured and stirred in his sleep that Shrick came out of his doorway. The keen blade with which he had slain Fat-Belly was grasped in both his hands. He launched himself towards the uneasy sleeper. His weapon sliced down once only – how often had he rehearsed this in his imagination! – and for the Thin-One the dream was over.

The smell of fresh blood, as always, excited him. It took him all of his will power to restrain himself from hacking and slashing at the dead Giant. But he promised himself that this would come later. And he jumped from the body of the Thin-One to where Loud-Voice was snoring noisily.

The abrupt cessation of that all too familiar sound must have awakened Bare-Head. Shrick saw him shift and stir, saw his hands go out to loosen the bonds that held him to his sleeping place. And when the Giant Killer, his feet scrabbling for a hold, landed on his chest he was ready. And he was shouting in a great Voice, so that Shrick knew that it was only a matter of heartbeats before the Little Giant came to his assistance.

Fat-Belly had been taken off guard, the Thin-One and Loud-Voice had been killed in their sleep. But here was no easy victory for the Giant Killer.

For a time it looked as though the chief of the Giants would win. After a little he ceased his shouting and fought with grim, silent desperation. Once one of his great hands caught Shrick in a bone-crushing grip, and it seemed as though the battle was over. Shrick could feel the blood pounding in his head, his eyeballs almost popping out of their sockets. It took him every ounce of resolution he possessed to keep from dropping his blade and scratching frenziedly at the other's wrist with in-effectual hands.

Something gave – it was his ribs – and in the fleeting instant of relaxed pressure he was able to twist, to turn and slash at the monstrous, hairy wrist. The warm blood spurted and the Giant cried aloud. Again and again Shrick plied his blade, until it became plain that the Giant would not be able to use that hand again.

He was single-handed now against an opponent as yet – insofar as his limbs were concerned – uncrippled. True, every movement of the upper part of his body brought spears of pain lancing through Shrick's chest. But he could move, and smite – and slay.

For Bare-Head weakened as the blood flowed from his wounds. No longer was he able to ward off the attacks on his face and neck. Yet he fought, as his race had always fought, to his dying breath. His enemy would have given no quarter – this much was obvious – but he could have sought refuge with the Little Giant in the Place-of-Little-Lights.

Towards the end he started shouting again.

And as he died, the Little Giant came into the cave.

It was sheer, blind luck that saved the Giant Killer from speedy death at the intruder's hands. Had the Little Giant known of the pitifully small forces arrayed against him it would have gone hard with Shrick. But No-Toes, left with her charges, had grown bored with the Place-of-Meeting. She had heard Shrick talk of the wonders of the Inside; and now, she thought, was her chance to see them for herself.

Followed by her charges she wandered aimlessly along the tunnels just outside the Barrier. She did not know the location of the doors to the Inside, and the view through the occasional peepholes was very circumscribed.

Then she came upon the doorway which Shrick had left open when he made his attack on the sleeping Giants. Bright light streamed through the aperture – light brighter than any No-Toes had seen before in her short life. Like a beacon it lured her on.

She did not hesitate when she came to the opening. Unlike her parents, she had not been brought up to regard the Giants with superstitious awe. Shrick was the only adult she could remember having known – and he, although he had talked of the Giants, had boasted of having slain one in single combat. He had said, also, that he would, at some time or other, kill all the Giants.

In spite of her lack of age and experience, No-Toes was no fool. Woman-like, already she had evaluated Shrick. Much of his talk she discounted as idle bragging, but she had never seen any reason to disbelieve his stories of the deaths of Big-Tusk, Sterrett, Tekka, Fat-Belly – and all the myriads of the People who had perished with them.

So it was that – foolhardy in her ignorance – she sailed through the doorway. Behind her came the other children, squealing in their excitement. Even if the Little Giant had not at first seen them he could not have failed to hear the shrill tumult of their irruption.

There was only one interpretation that he could put upon the evidence of his eyes. The plan to suffocate the People had failed. They had sallied out from their caves and tunnels to the massacre of his fellow Giants – and now fresh reinforcements were arriving to deal with him.

He turned and fled.

Shrick rallied his strength, made a flying leap from the monstrous carcass of Bare-Head. But in mid flight a hard, polished surface interposed itself between him and the fleeing Giant. Stunned, he hung against it for many heartbeats before he realized that it was a huge door which had shut in his face.

He knew that the Little Giant was not merely seeking refuge in flight – for where in the world could he hope to escape the wrath of the People ? He had gone, perhaps, for arms of some kind. Or – and at the thought Shrick's blood congealed – he had gone to loose the final doom foretold by Three-Eyes. Now that his plans had begun to miscarry he remembered the prophecy in its entirety, was no longer able to ignore those parts that, in his arrogance, he had found displeasing.

And then No-Toes, her flight clumsy and inexpert in these – to her – strange, vast spaces was at his side.

'Are you hurt ?' she gasped. 'They are so big – and you fought them.'

As she spoke, the world was filled with a deep humming sound. Shrick ignored the excited female. That noise could mean only one thing. The Little Giant was back in the Place-of-Little-Lights, was setting in motion vast, incomprehensible forces that would bring to pass the utter and irrevocable destruction of the People.

With his feet against the huge door he kicked off, sped rapidly down to the open doorway in the Barrier. He put out his hand to break the shock of his landing, screamed aloud as his impact sent a sickening wave of pain through his chest. He started to cough – and when he saw the bright blood that was welling from his mouth he was very frightened.

No-Toes was with him again. 'You are hurt, you are bleeding. Can I – ?'

'No!' he turned a snarling mask to her. 'No! Leave me alone!'

'But where are you going?'

Shrick paused. Then: 'I am going to save the world,' he said slowly. He savored the effect of his words. They made him feel better, they made him bulk big in his own mind, bigger, perhaps, than the Giants. 'I am going to save you all.'

'But how – ?'

This was too much for the Giant Killer. He screamed again, but this time with anger. With the back of his hand he struck the young female across the face.

'Stay here!' he ordered.

And then he was gone along the tunnel.

The gyroscopes were still singing their quiet song of power when Shrick reached the Control Room. Strapped in his chair, the navigator was busy over his plotting machine. Outside the ports the stars wheeled by in orderly succession.

And Shrick was frightened.

He had never quite believed Wesel's garbled version of the nature of the world until now. But he could see, at last, that the ship was moving. The fantastic wonder of it all held him spellbound until a thin edge of intolerable radiance crept into view from behind the rim of one of the ports. The navigator touched something and, suddenly, screens of dark blue glass mitigated the glare. But it was still bright, too bright, and the edge became a rapidly widening oval and then, at last, a disc.

The humming of the gyroscope stopped.

Before the silence had time to register a fresh sound assailed

Shrick's ears. It was the roar of the main drive.

A terrifying force seized him and slammed him down upon the deck. He felt his bones crack under the acceleration. True child of free fall as he was, all this held for him the terror of the supernatural. For a while he lay there, weakly squirming, whimpering a little. The navigator looked down at him and laughed. It was this sound more than anything else that stung Shrick to his last, supreme effort. He didn't want to move. He just wanted to lie there on the deck, slowly coughing his life away. But the Little Giant's derision tapped unsuspected reserves of strength, both moral and physical.

The navigator went back to his calculations, handling his instruments for the last time with a kind of desperate elation. He knew that the ship would never arrive at her destination, neither would her cargo of seed grain. But she would not – and this outweighed all other considerations – drift forever among the stars carrying within her hull the seeds of the destruction of Man and all his works.

He knew that – had he not taken this way out – he must have slept at last, and then death at the hands of the mutants would inevitably have been his portion. And with the mutants in full charge anything might happen.

The road he had taken was the best.

Unnoticed, inch by inch Shrick edged his way along the deck. Now, he could stretch his free hand and touch the Giant's foot. In the other he still held his blade, to which he had clung as the one thing sure and certain in this suddenly crazy world.

Then he had a grip on the artificial skin covering the Giant's leg. He started to climb, although every movement was un-adulterated agony. He did not see the other raise his hand to his mouth, swallow the little pellet that he held therein.

So it was that when, at long last, he reached the soft, smooth throat of the Giant, the Giant was dead.

It was a very fast poison.

For a while he clung there. He should have felt elation at the death of the last of his enemies but – instead – he felt cheated. There was so much that he wanted to know, so much that only

63

the Giants could have told him. Besides – it was his blade that should have won the final victory. He knew that, somewhere, the Little Giant was still laughing at him.

Through the blue-screened ports blazed the sun. Even at this distance, even with the intervening filters, its power and heat were all too evident. And aft the motors still roared, and would roar until the last ounce of fuel had been fed into the hungry main drive.

Shrick clung to the dead man's neck, looked long and longingly at the glittering instruments, the shining switches and levers, whose purpose he would never understand, whose inertia would have defeated any attempt of his fast ebbing strength to move them. He looked at the flaming doom ahead, and knew that this was what had been foretold.

Had the metaphor existed in his language, he would have told himself that he and the few surviving People were caught like rats in a trap.

But even the Giants would not have used that phrase in its metaphorical sense.

For that is all that the People were – rats in a trap.

THE BLACK DESTROYER

by A. E. van Vogt

On and on Coeurl prowled! The black, moonless, almost starless night yielded reluctantly before a grim reddish dawn that crept up from his left. A vague, dull light, it was, that gave no sense of approaching warmth, no comfort, nothing but a cold, diffuse lightness, slowly revealing a nighmare landscape.

Black, jagged rock and black, unliving plain took form around him, as a pale-red sun peered at last above the grotesque horizon. It was then Coeurl recognized suddenly that he was on familiar ground.

He stopped short. Tenseness flamed along his nerves. His muscles pressed with sudden, unrelenting strength against his bones. His great forelegs – twice as long as his hindlegs – twitched with a shuddering movement that arched every razor-sharp claw. The thick tentacles that sprouted from his shoulders ceased their weaving undulation, and grew taut with anxious alertness.

Utterly appalled, he twisted his great cat head from side to side, while the little hairlike tendrils that formed each ear vibrated frantically, testing every vagrant breeze, every throb in the ether.

But there was no response, no swift tingling along his intricate nervous system, not the faintest suggestion anywhere of the presence of the all-necessary id. Hopelessly, Coeurl crouched, an enormous catlike figure silhouetted against the dim reddish skyline, like a distorted etching of a black tiger resting on a black rock in a shadow world.

He had known this day would come. Through all the centuries of restless search, this day had loomed ever nearer, blacker, more frightening – this inevitable hour when he must return to the point where he began his systematic hunt in a world almost depleted of id-creatures.

The truth struck in waves like an endless, rhythmic ache at the seat of his ego. When he had started, there had been a few id-creatures in every hundred square miles, to be mercilessly rooted out. Only too well Coeurl knew in this ultimate hour that he had missed none. There were no id-creatures left to eat. In all the hundreds of thousands of square miles that he had made his own by right of ruthless conquest – until no neighboring coeurl dared to question his sovereignty – there was no id to feed the otherwise immortal engine that was his body.

Square foot by square foot he had gone over it. And now – he recognized the knoll of rock just ahead, and the black rock bridge that formed a queer, curling tunnel to his right. It was in that tunnel he had lain for days, waiting for the simple-minded, snakelike id-creature to come forth from its hole in the rock to bask in the sun – his first kill after he had realized the absolute necessity of organized extermination.

He licked his lips in brief gloating memory of the moment his slavering jaws tore the victim into precious toothsome bits. But the dark fear of an idless universe swept the sweet remembrance from his consciousness, leaving only certainty of death.

He snarled audibly, a defiant, devilish sound that quavered on the air, echoed and re-echoed among the rocks, and shuddered back along his nerves – instinctive and hellish expression of his will to live.

And then – abruptly – it came.

He saw it emerge out of the distance on a long downward slant, a tiny glowing spot that grew enormously into a metal ball. The great shining globe hissed by above Coeurl slowing visibly in quick deceleration. It sped over a black line of hills to the right, hovered almost motionless for a second, then sank down out of sight.

Coeurl exploded from his startled immobility. With tiger speed, he flowed down among the rocks. His round, black eyes burned with the horrible desire that was an agony within him. His ear tendrils vibrated a message of id in such tremendous quantities that his body felt sick with the pangs of his abnormal hunger.

The little red sun was a crimson ball in the purple-black heavens when he crept up from behind a mass of rock and gazed from its shadows at the crumbling, gigantic ruins of the city that sprawled below him. The silvery globe, in spite of its great size, looked strangely inconspicuous against that vast, fairylike reach of ruins. Yet about it was a leashed aliveness, a dynamic quiescence that, after a moment, made it stand out, dominating the foreground. A massive, rock-crushing thing of metal, it rested on a cradle made by its own weight in the harsh, resisting plain which began abruptly at the outskirts of the dead metropolis.

Coeurl gazed at the strange, two-legged creatures who stood in little groups near the brilliantly lighted opening that yawned at the base of the ship. His throat thickened with the immediacy of his need; and his brain grew dark with the first wild impulse to burst forth in furious charge and smash these flimsy, helpless-looking creatures whose bodies emitted the id-vibrations.

Mists of memory stopped that mad rush when it was still only electricity surging through his muscles. Memory that brought fear in an acid stream of weakness, pouring along his nerves, poisoning the reservoirs of his strength. He had time to see that the creatures wore things over their real bodies, shimmering transparent material that glittered in strange, burning flashes in the rays of the sun.

Other memories came suddenly. Of dim days when the city that spread below was the living, breathing heart of an age of glory that dissolved in a single century before flaming guns whose wielders knew only that for the survivors there would be an ever-narrowing supply of id.

It was the remembrance of those guns that held him there, cringing in a wave of terror that blurred his reason. He saw himself smashed by balls of metal and burned by searing flame.

Came cunning – understanding of the presence of these creatures. This, Coeurl reasoned for the first time, was a scientific expedition from another star. In the olden days, the coeurls had thought of space travel, but disaster came too swiftly for it ever to be more than a thought.

Scientists meant investigation, not destruction. Scientists in their way were fools. Bold with his knowledge, he emerged into the open. He saw the creatures become aware of him. They turned and stared. One, the smallest of the group, detached a shining metal rod from a sheath, and held it casually in one hand. Coeurl loped on, shaken to his core by the action; but it was too late to turn back.

Commander Hal Morton heard little Gregory Kent, the chemist, laugh with the embarrassed half gurgle with which he invariably announced inner uncertainty. He saw Kent fingering the spindly metalite weapon.

Kent said: 'I'll take no chances with anything as big as that.'

Commander Morton allowed his own deep chuckle to echo along the communicators. 'That,' he grunted finally, 'is one of the reasons why you're on this expedition, Kent – because you never leave anything to chance.'

His chuckle trailed off into silence. Instinctively, as he watched the monster approach them across that blackrock plain, he moved forward until he stood a little in advance of the others, his huge form bulking the transparent metalite suit. The comments of the men pattered through the radio communicator into his ears:

'I'd hate to meet that baby on a dark night in an ally.'

'Don't be silly. This is obviously an intelligent creature. Probably a member of the ruling race.'

'It looks like nothing else than a big cat, if you forget those tentacles sticking out from its shoulders, and make allowances for those monster forelegs.'

'Its physical development,' said a voice, which Morton recognized as that of Siedel, the psychologist, 'presupposes an animal-like adaptation to surroundings, not an intellectual one. On the other hand, its coming to us like this is not the act of an animal but of a creature possessing a mental awareness of our possible identity. You will notice that its movements are stiff, denoting caution, which suggests fear and consciousness of our

68

weapons. I'd like to get a good look at the end of its tentacles. If they taper into handlike appendages that can really grip objects, then the conclusion would be inescapable that it is a descendant of the inhabitants of this city. It would be a great help if we could establish communication with it, even though appearances indicate that it has degenerated into a historyless primitive.'

Coeurl stopped when he was still ten feet from the foremost creature. The sense of id was so overwhelming that his brain drifted to the ultimate verge of chaos. He felt as if his limbs were bathed in molten liquid; his very vision was not quite clear, as the sheer sensuality of his desire thundered through his being.

The men – all except the little one with the shining metal rod in his fingers – came closer. Coeurl saw that they were frankly and curiously examining him. Their lips were moving, and their voices beat in a monotonous, meaningless rhythm on his ear tendrils. At the same time he had the sense of waves of a much higher frequency – his own communication level – only it was a machinelike clicking that jarred his brain. With a distinct effort to appear friendly, he broadcast his name from his ear tendrils, at the same time pointing at himself with one curving tentacle.

Gourlay, chief of communications, drawled: 'I got a sort of static in my radio when he wiggled those hairs, Morton. Do you think –'

'Looks very much like it,' the leader answered the unfinished question. 'That means a job for you, Gourlay. If it speaks by means of radio waves, it might not be altogether impossible that you can create some sort of television picture of its vibrations, or teach him the Morse code.'

'Ah,' said Siedel. 'I was right. The tentacles each develop into seven strong fingers. Provided the nervous system is complicated enough, those fingers could, with training, operate any machine.' Morton said: 'I think we'd better go in and have some lunch. Afterward, we've got to get busy. The material men can set up their machines and start gathering data on the planet's metal possibilities, and so on. The others can do a little careful exploring. I'd like some notes on architecture and on the scientific development of this race, and particularly what happened to wreck the civilization. On earth civilization after civilization crumbled, but always a new one sprang up in its dust. Why didn't that happen here ? Any questions ?'

'Yes. What about kitty ? Look, he wants to come in with us.'

Commander Morton frowned, an action that emphasized the deep-space pallor of his face. 'I wish there was some way we could take it in with us, without forcibly capturing it. Kent, what do you think ?'

'I think we should first decide whether it's an it or a him, and call it one or the other. I'm in favor of him. As for taking him in with us –' The little chemist shook his head decisively. 'Impossible. This atmosphere is twenty-eight percent chlorine. Our oxygen would be pure dynamite to his lungs.'

The commander chuckled. 'He doesn't believe that, apparently.' He watched the catlike monster follow the first two men through the great door. The men kept an anxious distance from him, then glanced at Morton questioningly. Morton waved his hand. 'O.K. Open the second lock and let him get a whiff of the oxygen. That'll cure him.'

A moment later, he cursed his amazement. 'By Heaven, he doesn't even notice the difference! That means he hasn't any lungs, or else the chlorine is not what his lungs use. Let him in! You bet he can go in! Smith, here's a treasure house for a biologist – harmless enough if we're careful. We can always handle him. But what a metabolism!'

Smith, a tall, thin, bony chap with a long, mournful face, said in an oddly forceful voice: 'In all our travels, we've found only two higher forms of life. Those dependent on chlorine, and those who need oxygen – the two elements that support combustion. I'm prepared to stake my reputation that no complicated organism could ever adapt itself to both gases in a natural way. At first thought I should say here is an extremely advanced form of life. This race long ago discovered truths of biology that we are just beginning to suspect. Morton, we mustn't let this creature get away if we can help it.'

'If his anxiety to get inside is any criterion,' Commander

Morton laughed, 'then our difficulty will be to get rid of him.'

He moved into the lock with Coeurl and the two men. The automatic machinery hummed; and in a few minutes they were standing at the bottom of a series of elevators that led up to the living quarters.

'Does that go up?' One of the men flicked a thumb in the direction of the monster.

'Better send him up alone, if he'll go in.'

Coeurl offered no objection, until he heard the door slam behind him and the closed cage shot upward. He whirled with a savage snarl, his reason swirling into chaos. With one leap, he pounced at the door. The metal bent under his plunge, and the desperate pain maddened him. Now, he was all trapped animal. He smashed at the metal with his paws, bending it like so much tin. He tore great bars loose with his thick tentacles. The machinery screeched; there were horrible jerks as the limitless power pulled the cage along in spite of projecting pieces of metal that scraped the outside walls. And then the cage stopped, and he snatched off the rest of the door and hurtled into the corridor.

He waited there until Morton and the men came up with drawn weapons. 'We're fools,' Morton said. 'We should have shown him how it works. He thought we'd double-crossed him.'

He motioned to the monster, and saw the savage glow fade from the coal-black eyes as he opened and closed the door with elaborate gestures to show the operation.

Coeurl ended the lesson by trotting into the large room to his right. He lay down on the rugged floor, and fought down the electric tautness of his nerves and muscles. A very fury of rage against himself for his fright consumed him. It seemed to his burning brain that he had lost the advantage of appearing a mild and harmless creature. His strength must have startled and dismayed them.

It meant greater danger in the task which he now knew he must accomplish: To kill everything in the ship, and take the machine back to their world in search of unlimited id.

With unwinking eyes, Coeurl lay and watched the two men clearing away the loose rubble from the metal doorway of the huge old building. His whole body ached with the hunger of his cells for id. The craving tore through his palpitant muscles and throbbed like a living thing in his brain. His every nerve quivered to be off after the men who had wandered into the city. One of them, he knew, had gone – alone.

The dragging minutes fled; and still he restrained himself, still he lay there watching, aware that the men knew he watched. They floated a metal machine from the ship to the rock mass that blocked the great half-open door, under the direction of a third man. No flicker of their fingers escaped his fierce stare, and slowly, as the simplicity of the machinery became apparent to him, contempt grew upon him.

He knew what to expect finally, when the flame flared in incandescent violence and ate ravenously at the hard rock beneath. But in spite of his preknowledge, he deliberately jumped and snarled as if in fear, as that white heat burst forth. His ear tendrils caught the laughter of the men, their curious pleasure at his simulated dismay.

The door was released, and Morton came over and went inside with the third man. The latter shook his head.

'It's a shambles. You can catch the drift of the stuff. Obviously, they used atomic energy, but . . . but it's in wheel form. That's a peculiar development. In our science, atomic energy brought in the nonwheel machine. It's possible that here they've progressed *further* to a new type of wheel mechanics. I hope their libraries are better preserved than this, or we'll never know. What could have happened to a civilization to make it vanish like this ?'

A third voice broke through the communicators : 'This is Siedel. I heard your question, Pennons. Psychologically and sociologically speaking, the only reason why a territory becomes uninhabited is lack of food.'

'But they're so advanced scientifically, why didn't they develop space flying and go elsewhere for their food ?'

'Ask Gunlie Lester,' interjected Morton. 'I heard him expounding some theory even before we landed.'

The astronomer answered the first call. 'I've still got to verify all my facts, but this desolate world is the only planet revolving around that miserable red sun. There's nothing else. No moon, not even a planetoid. And the nearest star system is *nine hundred light-years* away.

'So tremendous would have been the problem of the ruling race of this world, that in one jump they would not only have had to solve interplanetary but interstellar space traveling. When you consider how slow our own development was – first the moon, then Venus – each success leading to the next, and after centuries to the nearest stars; and last of all to the anti-accelerators that permitted galactic travel. Considering all this, I maintain it would be impossible for any race to create such machines without practical experience. And, with the nearest star so far away, they had no incentive for the space adventuring that makes for experience.'

Coeurl was trotting briskly over to another group. But now, in the driving appetite that consumed him, and in the frenzy of his high scorn, he paid no attention to what they were doing. Memories of past knowledge, jarred into activity by what he had seen, flowed into his consciousness in an ever developing and more vivid stream.

From group to group he sped, a nervous dynamo – jumpy, sick with his awful hunger. A little car rolled up, stopping in front of him, and a formidable camera whirred as it took a picture of him. Over on a mound of rock, a gigantic telescope was staring up toward the sky. Nearby, a disintegrating machine drilled its searing fire into an ever-deepening hole, down and down, straight down.

Coeurl's mind became a blur of things he watched with half attention. And ever more imminent grew the moment when he knew he could no longer carry on the torture of acting. His brain strained with an irresistible impatience; his body burned with the fury of his eagerness to be off after the man who had gone alone into the city.

He could stand it no longer. A green foam misted his mouth, maddening him. He saw that, for the bare moment, nobody was looking.

Like a shot from a gun, he was off. He floated along in great, gliding leaps, a shadow among the shadows of the rocks. In a minute, the harsh terrain hid the spaceship and the two-legged beings.

Coeurl forgot the ship, forgot everything but his purpose, as if his brain had been wiped clear by a magic, memory-erasing brush. He circled widely, then raced into the city, along deserted streets, taking short cuts with the ease of familiarity, through gaping holes in time-weakened walls, through long corridors of moldering buildings. He slowed to a crouching lope as his ear tendrils caught the id vibrations.

Suddenly, he stopped and peered from a scatter of fallen rock. The man was standing at what must once have been a window, sending the glaring rays of his flashlight into the gloomy interior. The flashlight clicked off. The man, a heavy-set, powerful fellow, walked off with quick, alert steps. Coeurl didn't like that alertness. It presaged trouble; it meant lightning reaction to danger.

Coeurl waited till the human being had vanished around a corner, then he padded into the open. He was running now, tremendously faster than a man could walk, because his plan was clear in his brain. Like a wraith, he slipped down the next street, past a long block of buildings. He turned the first corner at top speed; and then, with dragging belly, crept into the hall-darkness between the building and a huge chunk of débris. The street ahead was barred by a solid line of loose rubble that made it like a valley, ending in a narrow, bottlelike neck. The neck had its outlet just below Coeurl.

His ear tendrils caught the low-frequency waves of whistling. The sound throbbed through his being; and suddenly terror caught with icy fingers at his brain. The man would have a gun. Suppose he leveled one burst of atomic energy – *one burst* – before his own muscles could whip out in murder fury.

A little shower of rocks streamed past. And then the man was beneath him. Coeurl reached out and struck a single crushing blow at the shimmering transparent headpiece of the space-suit. There was a tearing sound of metal and a gushing of blood. The man doubled up as if part of him had been telescoped. For a moment, his bones and legs and muscles combined miraculously to keep him standing. Then he crumpled with a metallic clank of his space armor.

Fear completely evaporated. Coeurl leaped out of hiding. With ravenous speed, he smashed the metal and the body within it to bits. Great chunks of metal, torn piecemeal from the suit, sprayed the ground. Bones cracked. Flesh crunched.

It was simple to tune in on the vibrations of the id, and to create the violent chemical disorganization that freed it from the crushed bone. The id was, Coeurl discovered, mostly in the bone.

He felt revived, almost reborn. Here was more food than he had had in the whole past year.

Three minutes, and it was over, and Coeurl was off like a thing fleeing dire danger. Cautiously, he approached the glistening globe from the opposite side to that by which he had left. The men were all busy at their tasks. Gliding noiselessly, Coeurl slipped unnoticed up to a group of men.

Morton stared down at the horror of tattered flesh, metal and blood on the rock at his feet, and felt a tightening in his throat that prevented speech. He heard Kent say:

'He *would* go alone, damn him!' The little chemist's voice held a sob imprisoned, and Morton remembered that Kent and Jarvey had chummed together for years in the way only two men can.

'The worst part of it is,' shuddered one of the men, 'it looks like a senseless murder. His body is spread out like little lumps of flattened jelly, but it seems to be all there. I'd almost wager there'd still be one hundred and seventy-five pounds by earth gravity. That'd be about one hundred and seventy pounds here.'

Smith broke in, his mournful face lined with gloom: 'The killer attacked Jarvey, and then discovered his flesh was alien – uneatable. Just like our big cat. Wouldn't eat anything we set before him –' His words died out in sudden, queer silence. Then he said slowly: 'Say, what about that creature? He's big enough and strong enough to have done this with his own little paws.'

Morton frowned. 'It's a thought. After all, he's the only living thing we've seen. We can't just execute him on suspicion, of course –'

'Besides,' said one of the men, 'he was never out of my sight.'

Before Morton could speak, Siedel, the psychologist, snapped, 'Positive about that ?'

The man hesitated. 'Maybe he was for a few minutes. He was wandering around so much, looking at everything.'

'Exactly,' said Siedel with satisfaction. He turned to Morton. 'You see, Commander, I, too, had the impression that he was always around; and yet thinking back over it, I find gaps. There were moments – probably long minutes – when he was completely out of sight.'

Morton's face was dark with thought, as Kent broke in fiercely: 'I say, take no chances. Kill the brute on suspicion before he does any more damage.'

Morton said slowly: 'Korita, you've been wandering around with Cranessy and Van Horne. Do you think kitty is a descendant of the ruling class of this planet ?'

The tall Japanese archeologist stared at the sky as if collecting his mind. 'Commander Morton,' he said finally, respectfully, 'there is a mystery here. Take a look, all of you, at the majestic skyline. Notice the almost Gothic outline of the architecture. In spite of the megalopolis which they created, these people were close to the soil. The buildings are not simply ornamented. They are ornamental in themselves. Here is the equivalent of the Doric column, the Egyptian pyramid, the Gothic cathedral, growing out of the ground, earnest, big with destiny. If this lonely, desolate world can be regarded as a mother earth, then the land had a warm, a spiritual place in the hearts of the race.

'The effect is emphasized by the winding streets. Their machines prove they were mathematicians, but they were artists first; and so they did not create the geometrically designed cities of the ultra-sophisticated world metropolis. There is a genuine artistic abandon, a deep joyous emotion

76

written in the curving and unmathematical arrangements of houses, buildings and avenues; a sense of intensity, of divine belief in an inner certainty. This is not a decadent, hoary-with-age civilization, but a young and vigorous culture, confident, strong with purpose.

'There it ended. Abruptly, as if at this point culture had its Battle of Tours, and began to collapse like the ancient Mohammedan civilization. Or as if in one leap it spanned the centuries and entered the period of contending states. In the Chinese civilization that period occupied 480–230 B.C., at the end of which the State of Tsin saw the beginning of the Chinese Empire. This phase Egypt experienced between 1780–1580 B.C., of which the last century was the "Hyksos" – unmentionable – time. The classical experienced it from Chaeronea – 338 – and, at the pitch of horror, from the Grachi – 133 – to Actium – 31 B.C. The West European Americans were devastated by it in the nineteenth and twentieth centuries, and modern historians agree that, nominally, we entered the same phase fifty years ago; though, of course, we have solved the problem.

'You may ask, Commander, what has all this to do with your question? My answer is: there is no record of a culture entering abruptly into the period of contending states. It is always a slow development; and the first step is a merciless questioning of all that was once held sacred. Inner certainties cease to exist, are dissolved before the ruthless probings of scientific and analytic minds. The skeptic becomes the highest type of being.

'I say that this culture ended abruptly in its most flourishing age. The sociological effects of such a catastrophe would be a sudden vanishing of morals, a reversion to almost bestial criminality, unleavened by any sense of ideal, a callous indifference to death. If this . . . this kitty is a descendant of such a race, then he will be a cunning creature, a thief in the night, a cold-blooded murderer, who would cut his own brother's throat for gain.'

'That's enough!' It was Kent's clipped voice. 'Commander, I'm willing to act the role of executioner.'

Smith interrupted sharply: 'Listen, Morton, you're not

going to kill that cat yet, even if he is guilty. He's a biological treasure house.'

Kent and Smith were glaring angrily at each other. Morton frowned at them thoughtfully, then said: 'Korita. I'm inclined to accept your theory as a working basis. But one question: Kitty comes from a period earlier than our own? That is, we are entering the highly civilized era of our culture, while he became suddenly historyless in the most vigorous period of his. *But* it is possible that his culture is a later one on this planet than ours is in the galactic-wide system we have civilized?'

'Exactly. His may be the middle of the tenth civilization of his world; while ours is the end of the eighth sprung from earth, each of the ten, of course, having been builded on the ruins of the one before it.'

'In that case, kitty would not know anything about the skepticism that made it possible for us to find him out so positively as a criminal and murderer?'

'No; it would be literally magic to him.'

Morton was smiling grimly. 'Then I think you'll get your wish, Smith. We'll let kitty live; and if there are any fatalities, now that we know him, it will be due to rank carelessness. There's just the chance, of course, that we're wrong. Like Siedel, I also have the impression that he was always around. But now – we can't leave poor Jarvey here like this. We'll put him in a coffin and bury him.'

'No, we won't!' Kent barked. He flushed. 'I beg your pardon, Commander. I didn't mean it that way. I maintain kitty wanted something from that body. It looks to be all there, but something must be missing. I'm going to find out what, and pin this murder on him so that you'll have to believe it beyond the shadow of a doubt.'

It was late night when Morton looked up from a book and saw Kent emerge through the door that led from the laboratories below.

Kent carried a large, flat bowl in his hands; his tired eyes flashed across at Morton, and he said in a weary, yet harsh, voice: 'Now watch!'

78

He started toward Coeurl, who lay sprawled on the great rug, pretending to be asleep.

Morton stopped him. 'Wait a minute, Kent. Any other time, I wouldn't question your actions, but you look ill; you're overwrought. What have you got there?'

Kent turned, and Morton saw that his first impression had been but a flashing glimpse of the truth. There were dark pouches under the little chemist's gray eyes – eyes that gazed feverishly from sunken cheeks in an ascetic face.

'I've found the missing element,' Kent said. 'It's phosphorus. There wasn't so much as a square millimeter of phosphorus left in Jarvey's bones. Every bit of it had been drained out – by what superchemistry I don't know. There are ways of getting phosphorus out of the human body. For instance, a quick way was what happened to the workman who helped build this ship. Remember, he fell into fifteen tons of molten metalite – at least, so his relatives claimed – but the company wouldn't pay compensation until the metalite, on analysis, was found to contain a high percentage of phosphorus –'

'What about the bowl of food?' somebody interrupted. Men were putting away magazines and books, looking up with interest.

'It's got organic phosphorus in it. He'll get the scent, or whatever it is that he uses instead of scent –'

'I think he gets the vibrations of things,' Gourlay interjected lazily. 'Sometimes, when he wiggles those tendrils, I get a distinct static on the radio. And then, again, there's no reaction, just as if he's moved higher or lower on the wave scale. He seems to control the vibrations at will.'

Kent waited with obvious impatience until Gourlay's last word, then abruptly went on: 'All right, then, when he gets the vibration of the phosphorus and reacts to it like an animal, then – well, we can decide what we've proved by his reaction. Can I go ahead, Morton?'

'There are three things wrong with your plan,' Morton said. 'In the first place, you seem to assume that he is only animal; you seem to have forgotten he may not be hungry after Jarvey; you seem to think that he will not be suspicious. But set the

79

bowl down. His reaction may tell us something.'

Coeurl stared with unblinking black eyes as the man set the bowl before him. His ear tendrils instantly caught the id-vibrations from the contents of the bowl – and he gave it not even a second glance.

He recognized this two-legged being as the one who had held the weapon that morning. Danger! With a snarl, he floated to his feet. He caught the bowl with the fingerlike appendages at the end of one looping tentacle, and emptied its contents into the face of Kent, who shrank back with a yell.

Explosively, Coeurl flung the bowl aside and snapped a hawser-thick tentacle around the cursing man's waist. He didn't bother with the gun that hung from Kent's belt. It was only a vibration gun, he sensed – atomic powered, but not an atomic disintegrator. He tossed the kicking Kent onto the nearest couch – and realized with a hiss of dismay that he should have disarmed the man.

Not that the gun was dangerous – but, as the man furiously wiped the gruel from his face with one hand, he reached with the other for his weapon. Coeurl crouched back as the gun was raised slowly and a white beam of flame was discharged at his massive head.

His ear tendrils hummed as they canceled the efforts of the vibration gun. His round, black eyes narrowed as he caught the movement of men reaching for their metalite guns. Morton's voice lashed across the silence.

'Stop!'

Kent clicked off his weapon; and Coeurl crouched down, quivering with fury at this man who had forced him to reveal something of his power.

'Kent,' said Morton coldly, 'you're not the type to lose your head. You deliberately tried to kill kitty, knowing that the majority of us are in favor of keeping him alive. You know what our rule is: If anyone objects to my decisions, he must say so *at the time*. If the majority object, my decisions are overruled. In this case, no one but you objected, and, therefore, your action in taking the law into your own hands is most reprehensible, and automatically debars you from voting for a year.'

Kent stared grimly at the circle of faces. 'Korita was right when he said ours was a highly civilized age. It's decadent.' Passion flamed harshly in his voice. 'My God, isn't there a man here who can see the horror of the situation? Jarvey dead only a few hours, and this creature, whom we all know to be guilty, lying there unchained, planning his next murder; and the victim is right here in this room. What kind of men are we – fools, cynics, ghouls – or is it that our civilization is so steeped in reason that we can contemplate a murder sympathetically?'

He fixed brooding eyes on Coeurl. 'You were right, Morton, that's no animal. That's a devil from the deepest hell of this planet, whirling its solitary way around a dying sun.'

'Don't go melodramatic on us,' Morton said. 'Your analysis is all wrong, so far as I am concerned. We're not ghouls or cynics; we're simply scientists, and kitty here is going to be studied. Now that we suspect him, we doubt his ability to trap any of us. One against a hundred hasn't a chance.' He glanced around. 'Do I speak for all of us?'

'Not for me, commander!' It was Smith who spoke, and, as Morton stared in amazement, he continued: 'In the excitement and momentary confusion, no one seems to have noticed that when Kent fired his vibration gun, the beam hit this creature squarely on his cat head – and didn't hurt him.'

Morton's amazed glance went from Smith to Coeurl, and back to Smith again. 'Are you certain it hit him? As you say, it all happened so swiftly – when kitty wasn't hurt I simply assumed that Kent had missed him.'

'He hit him in the face,' Smith said positively. 'A vibration gun, of course, can't even kill a man right away – but it can injure him. There's no sign of injury on kitty, though, not even a singed hair.'

'Perhaps his skin is a good insulation against heat of any kind.'

'Perhaps. But in view of our uncertainty, I think we should lock him up in the cage.'

While Morton frowned darkly in thought, Kent spoke up. 'Now you're talking sense, Smith.'

Morton asked: 'Then you would be satisfied, Kent, if we put

him in the cage?'

Kent considered, finally: 'Yes. If four inches of micro-steel can't hold him, we'd better give him the ship.'

Coeurl followed the men as they went out into the corridor. He trotted docilely along as Morton unmistakably motioned him through a door he had not hitherto seen. He found himself in a square solid metal room. The door clanged metallically behind him; he felt the flow of power as the electric lock clicked home.

His lips parted in a grimace of hate, as he realized the trap, but he gave no other outward reaction. It occurred to him that he had progressed a long way from the sunk-into-primitiveness creature who, a few hours before, had gone incoherent with fear in an elevator cage. Now, a thousand memories of his powers were reawakened in his brain; ten thousand cunnings were, after ages of disuse, once again part of his very being.

He sat quite still for a moment on the short, heavy haunches into which his body tapered, his ear tendrils examining his surroundings. Finally, he lay down, his eyes glowing with contemptuous fire. The fools! The poor fools!

It was about an hour later when he heard the man – Smith – fumbling overhead. Vibrations poured upon him, and for just an instant he was startled. He leaped to his feet in pure terror – and then realized that the vibrations *were* vibrations, not atomic explosions. Somebody was taking pictures of the inside of his body.

He crouched down again, but his ear tendrils vibrated, and he thought contemptuously: the silly fool would be surprised when he tried to develop those pictures.

After a while the man went away, and for a long time there were noises of men doing things far away. That, too, died away slowly.

Coeurl lay waiting, as he felt the silence creep over the ship. In the long ago, before the dawn of immortality, the coeurls, too, had slept at night; and the memory of it had been revived the day before when he saw some of the men dozing. At last, the vibration of two pairs of feet, pacing, pacing endlessly, was the only human-made frequency that throbbed on his ear tendrils.

Tensely, he listened to the two watchmen. The first one walked slowly past the cage door. Then about thirty feet behind him came the second. Coeurl sensed the alertness of these men; knew that he could never surprise either while they walked separately. It meant – he must be doubly careful!

Fifteen minutes, and they came again. The moment they were past, he switched his senses from their vibrations to a vastly higher range. The pulsating violence of the atomic engines stammered its soft story to his brain. The electric dynamos hummed their muffled song of pure power. He felt the whisper of that flow through the wires in the walls of his cage, and through the electric lock of his door. He forced his quivering body into straining immobility, his senses seeking, searching, to tune in on that sibilant tempest of energy. Suddenly, his ear tendrils vibrated in harmony – he caught the surging change into shrillness of that rippling force wave.

There was a sharp click of metal on metal. With a gentle touch of one tentacle, Coeurl pushed open the door, and glided out into the dully gleaming corridor. For just a moment, he felt contempt, a glow of superiority, as he thought of the stupid creatures who dared to match their wit against a coeurl. And in that moment, he suddenly thought of other coeurls. A queer, exultant sense of race pounded through his being; the driving hate of centuries of ruthless competition yielded reluctantly before pride of kinship with the future rulers of all space.

Suddenly, he felt weighed down by his limitations, his need for other coeurls, his aloneness – one against a hundred, with the stake all eternity; the starry universe itself beckoned his rapacious, vaulting ambition. If he failed, there would never be a second chance – no time to revive long-rotted machinery, and attempt to solve the secret of space travel.

He padded along on tensed paws – through the salon – into the next corridor – and came to the first bedroom door. It stood half open. One swift flow of synchronized muscles, one swiftly lashing tentacle that caught the unresisting throat of the sleeping man, crushing it; and the lifeless head rolled crazily, the body twitched once.

Seven bedrooms; seven dead men. It was the seventh taste of murder that brought a sudden return of lust, a pure, unbounded desire to kill, return of a millennium-old habit of destroying everything containing the precious id.

As the twelfth man slipped convulsively into death, Coeurl emerged abruptly from the sensuous joy of the kill to the sound of footsteps.

They were not near – that was what brought wave after wave of fright swirling into the chaos that suddenly became his brain.

The watchmen were coming slowly along the corridor toward the door of the cage where he had been imprisoned. In a moment, the first man would see the open door – and sound the alarm.

Coeurl caught at the vanishing remnants of his reason. With frantic speed, careless now of accidental sounds, he raced – along the corridor with its bedroom doors – through the salon. He emerged into the next corridor, cringing in awful anticipation of the atomic flame he expected would stab into his face.

The two men were together, standing side by side. For one single instant, Coeurl could scarcely believe his tremendous good luck. Like a fool the second had come running when he saw the other stop before the open door. They looked up, paralyzed, before the nightmare of claws and tentacles, the ferocious cat head and hate-filled eyes.

The first man went for his gun, but the second, physically frozen before the doom he saw, uttered a shriek, a shrill cry of horror that floated along the corridors – and ended in a curious gurgle, as Coeurl flung the two corpses with one irresistible motion the full length of the corridor. He didn't want the dead bodies found near the cage. That was his one hope.

Shaking in every nerve and muscle, conscious of the terrible error he had made, unable to think coherently, he plunged into the cage. The door clicked softly shut behind him. Power flowed once more through the electric lock.

He crouched tensely, simulating sleep, as he heard the rush of many feet, caught the vibration of excited voices. He knew when somebody actuated the cage audioscope and looked in. A few moments now, and the other bodies would be discovered.

'Siedel gone!' Morton said numbly. 'What are we going to do without Siedel? And Breckenridge! And Coulter and – Horrible!'

He covered his face with his hands, but only for an instant. He looked up grimly, his heavy chin outthrust as he stared into the stern faces that surrounded him. 'If anybody's got so much as a germ of an idea, bring it out.'

'Space madness!'

'I've thought of that. But there hasn't been a case of a man going mad for fifty years. Dr. Eggert will test everybody, of course, and right now he's looking at the bodies with that possibility in mind.'

As he finished, he saw the doctor coming through the door. Men crowded aside to make way for him.

'I heard you, Commander,' Dr. Eggert said, 'and I think I can say right now that the space-madness theory is out. The throats of these men have been squeezed to a jelly. No human being could have exerted such enormous strength without using a machine.'

Morton saw that the doctor's eyes kept looking down the corridor, and he shook his head and groaned:

'It's no use suspecting kitty, doctor. He's in his cage, pacing up and down. Obviously heard the racket and – Man alive! You can't suspect him. That cage was built to hold literally *anything* – four inches of micro-steel – and there's not a scratch on the door. Kent, even you won't say, "Kill him on suspicion," because there can't be any suspicion, unless there's a new science here, beyond anything we can imagine –'

'On the contrary,' said Smith flatly, 'we have all the evidence we need. I used the telefluor on him – you know the arrangement we have on top of the cage – and tried to take some pictures. They just blurred. Kitty jumped when the telefluor was turned on, as if he felt the vibrations.

'You all know what Gourlay said before? This beast can apparently receive and send vibrations of any lengths. The way he dominated the power of Kent's gun is final proof of his special ability to interfere with energy.'

'What in the name of all the hells have we got here?' One of the men groaned. 'Why, if he can control that power, and send it out in any vibrations, there's nothing to stop him killing all of us.'

'Which proves,' snapped Morton, 'that he isn't invincible, or he would have done it long ago.'

Very deliberately, he walked over to the mechanism that controlled the prison cage.

'You're not going to open the door!' Kent gasped, reaching for his gun.

'No, but if I pull this switch, electricity will flow through the floor, and electrocute whatever's inside. We've never had to use this before, so you had probably forgotten about it.'

He jerked the switch hard over. Blue fire flashed from the metal, and a bank of fuses above his head exploded with a single bang.

Morton frowned. 'That's funny. Those fuses shouldn't have blown! Well, we can't even look in, now. That wrecked the audios, too.'

Smith said: 'If he could interfere with the electric lock, enough to open the door, then he probably probed every possible danger and was ready to interfere when you threw that switch.'

'At least, it proves he's vulnerable to our energies!' Morton smiled grimly. 'Because he rendered them harmless. The important thing is, we've got him behind four inches of the toughest of metal. At the worse we can open the door and ray him to death. But first, I think we'll try to use the telefluor power cable –'

A commotion from inside the cage interrupted his words. A heavy body crashed against a wall, followed by a dull thump.

'He knows what we were trying to do!' Smith grunted to Morton. 'And I'll bet it's a very sick kitty in there. What a fool he was to go back into that cage and does he realize it!'

The tension was relaxing; men were smiling nervously, and there was even a ripple of humorless laughter at the picture Smith drew of the monster's discomfiture.

'What I'd like to know,' said Pennons, the engineer, 'is, why did the telefluor meter dial jump and waver at full power when kitty made that noise? It's right under my nose here, and the dial jumped like a house afire!'

There was silence both without and within the cage, then Morton said: 'It may mean he's coming out. Back, everybody, and keep your guns ready. Kitty was a fool to think he could conquer a hundred men, but he's by far the most formidable creature in the galactic system. He may come out of that door, rather than die like a rat in a trap. And he's just tough enough to take some of us with him – if we're not careful.'

The men backed slowly in a solid body; and somebody said: 'That's funny. I thought I heard the elevator.'

'Elevator!' Morton echoed. 'Are you sure, man?'

'Just for a moment I was!' The man, a member of the crew, hesitated. 'We were all shuffling our feet –'

'Take somebody with you, and go look. Bring whoever dared to run off back here –'

There was a jar, a horrible jerk, as the whole gigantic body of the ship careened under them. Morton was flung to the floor with a violence that stunned him. He fought back to consciousness, aware of the other men lying all around him. He shouted: 'Who the devil started those engines!'

The agonizing acceleration continued; his feet dragged with awful exertion, as he fumbled with the nearest audioscope, and punched the engine-room number. The picture that flooded onto the screen brought a deep bellow to his lips:

'It's kitty! He's in the engine room – and we're heading straight out into space.'

The screen went black even as he spoke, and he could see no more.

It was Morton who first staggered across the salon floor to the supply room where the spacesuits were kept. After fumbling almost blindly into his own suit, he cut the effects of the body-torturing acceleration, and brought suits to the semi-conscious men on the floor. In a few moments, other men were assisting him; and then it was only a matter of minutes before everybody was clad in metalite, with anti-acceleration motors running at half power.

It was Morton then who, after first looking into the cage, opened the door and stood, silent as the others crowded about him, to stare at the gaping hole in the rear wall. The hole was a frightful thing of jagged edges and horribly bent metal, and it opened upon another corridor.

'I'll swear,' whispered Pennons, 'that it's impossible. The ten-ton hammer in the machine shops couldn't more than dent four inches of micro with one blow – and we only heard one. It would take at least a minute for an atomic disintegrator to do the job. Morton, this is a super-being.'

Morton saw that Smith was examining the break in the wall. The biologist looked up. 'If only Breckenridge weren't dead! We need a metallurgist to explain this. Look!'

He touched the broken edge of the metal. A piece crumbled in his finger and slithered away in a fine shower of dust to the floor. Morton noticed for the first time that there was a little pile of metallic débris and dust.

'You've hit it.' Morton nodded. 'No miracle of strength here. The monster merely used his special powers to interfere with the electronic tensions holding the metal together. That would account, too, for the drain on the telefluor power cable that Pennons noticed. The thing used the power with his body as a transforming medium, smashed through the wall, ran down the corridor to the elevator shaft, and so down to the engine room.'

'In the meantime, Commander,' Kent said quietly, 'we are faced with a super-being in control of the ship, completely dominating the engine room, and its almost unlimited power, and in possession of the best part of the machine shops.'

Morton felt the silence, while the men pondered the chemist's words. Their anxiety was a tangible thing that lay heavily upon their faces; in every expression was the growing realization that here was the ultimate situation in their lives; their very existence was at stake, and perhaps much more. Morton voiced the thought in everybody's mind:

'Suppose he wins. He's utterly ruthless, and he probably sees galactic power within his grasp.'

'Kent is wrong,' barked the chief navigator. 'The thing

doesn't dominate the engine room. We've still got the control room, and that gives us *first* control of all the machines. You fellows may not know the mechanical set-up we have; but, though he can eventually disconnect us, we can cut off all the switches in the engine room *now*. Commander, why didn't you just shut off the power instead of putting us into spacesuits? At the very least you could have adjusted the ship to the acceleration.'

'For two reasons,' Morton answered. 'Individually, we're safer within the force fields of our spacesuits. And we can't afford to give up our advantages in panicky moves.'

'Advantages. What other advantages have we got?'

'We know things about him,' Morton replied. 'And right now, we're going to make a test. Pennons, detail five men to each of the four approaches to the engine room. Take atomic disintegrators to blast through the big doors. They're all shut, I noticed. He's locked himself in.

'Selenski, you go up to the control room and shut off everything except the drive engines. Gear them to the master switch, and shut them off all at once. One thing, though – leave the acceleration on full blast. No anti-acceleration must be applied to the ship. Understand?'

'Aye, sir!' The pilot saluted.

'And report to me through the communicators if any of the machines start to run again.' He faced the men. 'I'm going to lead the main approach. Kent, you take No. 2; Smith, No. 3; and Pennons, No. 4. We're going to find out right now if we're dealing with unlimited science, or a creature limited like the rest of us. I'll bet on the last possibility.'

Morton had an empty sense of walking endlessly, as he moved, a giant of a man in his transparent space armor, along the glistening metal tube that was the main corridor of the engine room floor. Reason told him the creature had already shown feet of clay, yet the feeling that here was an invincible being persisted.

He spoke into the communicator: 'It's no use trying to sneak up on him. He can probably hear a pin drop. So just wheel up your units. He hasn't been in that engine room long enough to do anything.

'As I've said, this is largely a test attack. In the first place, we could never forgive ourselves if we didn't try to conquer him now, before he's had time to prepare against us. But, aside from the possibility that we can destroy him immediately, I have a theory.

'The idea goes something like this: Those doors are built to withstand accidental atomic explosions, and it will take fifteen minutes for the atomic disintegrators to smash them. During that period the monster will have no power. True, the drive will be on, but that's straight atomic explosion. My theory is, he can't touch stuff like that; and in a few minutes you'll see what I mean – I hope.'

His voice was suddenly crisp: 'Ready, Selenski?'

'Aye, ready.'

'Then cut the master switch.'

The corridor – the whole ship, Morton knew – was abruptly plunged into darkness. Morton clicked on the dazzling light of his spacesuit; the other men did the same, their faces pale and drawn.

'Blast!' Morton barked into his communicator.

The mobile units throbbed; and then pure atomic flame ravened out and poured upon the hard metal of the door. The first molten droplet rolled reluctantly, not down, but up the door. The second was more normal. It followed a shaky downward course. The third rolled sideways – for this was pure force, not subject to gravitation. Other drops followed until a dozen streams trickled sedately yet unevenly in every direction – streams of hellish, sparkling fire, bright as fairy gems, alive with the coruscating fury of atoms suddenly tortured, and running blindly, crazy with pain.

The minutes ate at time like a slow acid. At last Morton asked huskily:

'Selenski?'

'Nothing yet, Commander.'

Morton half whispered: 'But he must be doing something. He can't be just waiting in there like a cornered rat. Selenski?'

'Nothing, Commander.'

Seven minutes, eight minutes, then twelve.

'Commander!' It was Selenski's voice, taut. 'He's got the electric dynamo running.'

Morton drew a deep breath, and heard one of his men say:

'That's funny. We can't get any deeper. Boss, take a look at this.'

Morton looked. The little scintillating streams had frozen rigid. The ferocity of the disintegrators vented in vain against metal grown suddenly invulnerable.

Morton sighed. 'Our test is over. Leave two men guarding every corridor. The others come up to the control room.'

He seated himself a few minutes later before the massive control keyboard. 'So far as I'm concerned the test was a success. We know that of all the machines in the engine room, the most important to the monster was the electric dynamo. He must have worked in a frenzy of terror while we were at the doors.'

'Of course, it's easy to see what he did,' Pennons said. 'Once he had the power he increased the electronic tensions of the door to their ultimate.'

'The main thing is this,' Smith chimed in. 'He works with vibrations only so far as his special powers are concerned, and the energy must come from outside himself. Atomic energy in its pure form, not being vibration, he can't handle any differently than we can.'

Kent said glumly: 'The main point in my opinion is that he stopped us cold. What's the good of knowing that his control over vibrations did it? If we can't break through those doors with our atomic disintegrators, we're finished.'

Morton shook his head. 'Not finished – but we'll have to do some planning. First though, I'll start these engines. It'll be harder for him to get control of them when they're running.'

He pulled the master switch back into place with a jerk. There was a hum, as scores of machines leaped into violent life in the engine room a hundred feet below. The noises sank to a steady vibration of throbbing power.

Three hours later, Morton paced up and down before the men gathered in the salon. His dark hair was uncombed; the space pallor of his strong face emphasized rather than detracted from the outthrust aggressiveness of his jaw. When he spoke, his deep voice was crisp to the point of sharpness:

'To make sure that our plans are fully co-ordinated, I'm going to ask each expert in turn to outline his part in the overpowering of this creature. Pennons first!'

Pennons stood up briskly. He was not a big man, Morton thought, yet he looked big, perhaps because of his air of authority. This man knew engines, and the history of engines. Morton had heard him trace a machine through its evolution from a simple toy to the highly complicated modern instrument. He had studied machine development on a hundred planets; and there was literally nothing fundamental that he didn't know about mechanics. It was almost weird to hear Pennons, who could have spoken for a thousand hours and still only have touched upon his subject, say with absurd brevity:

'We've set up a relay in the control room to start and stop every engine rhythmically. The trip lever will work a hundred times a second, and the effect will be to create vibrations of every description. There is just a possibility that one or more of the machines will burst, on the principle of soldiers crossing a bridge in step – you've heard that old story, no doubt – but in my opinion there is no real danger of a break of that tough metal. The main purpose is simply to interfere with the interference of the creature, and smash through the doors.'

'Gourlay next!' barked Morton.

Gourlay climbed lazily to his feet. He looked sleepy, as if he was somewhat bored by the whole proceedings, yet Morton knew he loved people to think him lazy, a good-for-nothing slouch, who spent his days in slumber and his nights catching forty winks. His title was chief communication engineer, but his knowledge extended to every vibration field; and he was probably, with the possible exception of Kent, the fastest thinker on the ship. His voice drawled out, and – Morton noted – the very deliberate assurance of it had a soothing effect on the men – anxious faces relaxed, bodies leaned back more restfully:

'Once inside,' Gourlay said, 'we've rigged up vibration

screens of pure force that should stop nearly everything he's got on the ball. They work on the principle of reflection, so that everything he sends will be reflected back to him. In addition, we've got plenty of spare electric energy that we'll just feed him from mobile copper cups. There must be a limit to his capacity for handling power with those insulated nerves of his.'

'Selenski!' called Morton.

The chief pilot was already standing, as if he had anticipated Morton's call. And that, Morton reflected, was the man. His nerves had that rocklike steadiness which is the first requirement of the master controller of a great ship's movements; yet that very steadiness seemed to rest on dynamite ready to explode at its owner's volition. He was not a man of great learning, but he 'reacted' to stimuli so fast that he always seemed to be anticipating.

'The impression I've received of the plan is that it must be cumulative. Just when the creature thinks that he can't stand any more, another thing happens to add to his trouble and confusion. When the uproar's at its height, I'm supposed to cut in the anti-accelerators. The commander thinks with Gunlie Lester that these creatures will know nothing about anti-acceleration. It's a development, pure and simple, of the science of interstellar flight, and couldn't have been developed in any other way. We think when the creature feels the first effects of the anti-acceleration – you all remember the caved-in feeling you had the first month – it won't know what to think or do.'

'Korita next.'

'I can only offer you encouragement,' said the archaeologist, 'on the basis of my theory that the monster has all the characteristics of a criminal of the early ages of any civilization, complicated by an apparent reversion to primitive..ess. The suggestion has been made by Smith that his knowledge of science is puzzling, and could only mean that we are dealing with an actual inhabitant, not a descendant of the inhabitants of the dead city we visited. This would ascribe a virtual immortality to our enemy, a possibility which is borne out by his ability to breathe both oxygen and chlorine – or neither – but even that makes no difference. He comes from a certain age in his civilization; and he has sunk so low that his ideas are mostly memories of that age.

'In spite of all the powers of his body, he lost his head in the elevator the first morning, until he remembered. He placed himself in such a position that he was forced to reveal his special powers against vibrations. He bungled the mass murders a few hours ago. In fact, his whole record is one of the low cunning of the primitive, egotistical mind which has little or no conception of the vast organization with which it is confronted.

'He is like the ancient German soldier who felt superior to the elderly Roman scholar, yet the latter was part of a mighty civilization of which the Germans of that day stood in awe.

'You may suggest that the sack of Rome by the Germans in later years defeats my argument; however, modern historians agree that the "sack" was an historical accident, and not history in the true sense of the word. The movement of the "Sea-peoples" which set in against the Egyptian civilization from 1400 B.C. succeeded only as regards the Cretan island-realm – their mighty expeditions against the Libyan and Phœnician coasts, with the accompaniment of viking fleets, failed as those of the Huns failed against the Chinese Empire. Rome would have been abandoned in any event. Ancient, glorious Samarra was desolate by the tenth century; Patali-putra, Asoka's great capital, was an immense and completely uninhabited waste of houses when the Chinese traveler Hsinan-tang visited it about A.D. 635.

'We have, then, a primitive, and that primitive is now far out in space, completely outside of his natural habitat. I say, let's go in and win.'

One of the men grumbled, as Korita finished: 'You can talk about the sack of Rome being an accident, and about this fellow being a primitive, but the facts are facts. It looks to me as if Rome is about to fall again; and it won't be no primitive that did it, either. This guy's got plenty of what it takes.'

Morton smiled grimly at the man, a member of the crew. 'We'll see about that – right now!'

In the blazing brilliance of the gigantic machine shop, Coeurl slaved. The forty-foot, cigar-shaped spaceship was nearly finished. With a grunt of effort, he completed the laborious installation of the drive engines, and paused to survey his craft.

Its interior, visible through the one aperture in the outer wall, was pitifully small. There was literally room for nothing but the engines – and a narrow space for himself.

He plunged frantically back to work as he heard the approach of the men, and the sudden change in the tempest-like thunder of the engines – a rhythmical off-and-on hum, shriller in tone, sharper, more nerve-racking than the deep-throated, steady throb that had preceded it. Suddenly, there were the atomic disintegrators again at the massive outer doors.

He fought them off, but never wavered from his task. Every mighty muscle of his powerful body strained as he carried great loads of tools, machines and instruments, and dumped them into the bottom of his makeshift ship. There was no time to fit anything into place, no time for anything – no time – no time.

The thought pounded at his reason. He felt strangely weary for the first time in his long and vigorous existence. With a last, tortured heave, he jerked the gigantic sheet of metal into the gaping aperture of the ship – and stood there for a terrible minute balancing it precariously.

He knew the doors were going down. Half a dozen disintegrators concentrating on one point were irresistibly, though slowly, eating away the remaining inches. With a gasp, he released his mind from the doors and concentrated every ounce of his mind on the yard-thick outer wall, toward which the blunt nose of his ship was pointing.

His body cringed from the surging power that flowed from the electric dynamo through his ear tendrils into that resisting wall. The whole inside of him felt on fire, and he knew that he was dangerously close to carrying his ultimate load.

And still he stood there, shuddering with the awful pain, holding the unfastened metal plate with hard-clenched tentacles. His massive head pointed as in dread fascination at that bitterly hard wall.

He heard one of the engine-room doors crash inward. Men

shouted; disintegrators rolled forward, their raging power unchecked. Coeurl heard the floor of the engine room hiss in protest, as those beams of atomic energy tore everything in their path to bits. The machines rolled closer; cautious footsteps sounded behind them. In a minute they would be at the flimsy doors separating the engine room from the machine shop.

Suddenly, Coeurl was satisfied. With a snarl of hate, a vindictive glow of feral eyes, he ducked into his little craft, and pulled the metal plate down into place as if it was a hatchway.

His ear tendrils hummed, as he softened the edges of the surrounding metal. In an instant, the plate was more than welded – it was part of his ship, a seamless, rivetless part of a whole that was solid opaque metal except for two transparent areas, one in the front, one in the rear.

His tentacles embraced the power drive with almost sensuous tenderness. There was a forward surge of his fragile machine, straight at the great outer wall of the machine shops. The nose of the forty-foot craft touched – and the wall dissolved in a glittering shower of dust.

Coeurl felt the barest retarding movement; and then he kicked the nose of the machine out into the cold of space, twisted it about, and headed back in the direction from which the big ship had been coming all these hours.

Men in space armor stood in the jagged hole that yawned in the lower reaches of the gigantic globe. The men and the great ship grew smaller. Then the men were gone; and there was only the ship with its blaze of a thousand blurring portholes. The ball shrank incredibly, too small now for individual portholes to be visible.

Almost straight ahead, Coeurl saw a tiny, dim, reddish ball – his own sun, he realized. He headed toward it at full speed. There were caves where he could hide and with other coeurls build secretly a spaceship in which they could reach other planets safely – now that he knew how.

His body ached from the agony of acceleration, yet he dared not let up for a single instant. He glanced back, half in terror. The globe was still there, a tiny dot of light in the immense blackness of space. Suddenly it twinkled and was gone.

For a brief moment, he had the empty, frightened impression that just before it disappeared, it moved. But he could see nothing. He could not escape the belief that they had shut off all their lights, and were sneaking up on him in the darkness. Worried and uncertain, he looked through the forward transparent plate.

A tremor of dismay shot through him. The dim red sun toward which he was heading was not growing larger. *It was becoming smaller* by the instant. And it grew visibly tinier during the next five minutes, became a pale-red dot in the sky – and vanished like the ship.

Fear came then, a blinding surge of it, that swept through his being and left him chilled with the sense of the unknown. For minutes, he stared frantically into the space ahead, searching for some landmark. But only the remote stars glimmered there, unwinking points against a velvet background of unfathomable distance.

Wait! One of the points was growing larger. With every muscle and nerve tensed, Coeurl watched the point becoming a dot, a round ball of light – red light. Bigger, bigger, it grew. Suddenly, the red light shimmered and turned white – and there, before him, was the great globe of the spaceship, lights glaring from every porthole, the very ship which a few minutes before he had watched vanish behind him.

Something happened to Coeurl in that moment. His brain was spinning like a flywheel, faster, faster, more incoherently. Suddenly, the wheel flew apart into a million aching fragments. His eyes almost started from their sockets as, like a maddened animal, he raged in his small quarters.

His tentacles clutched at precious instruments and flung them insensately; his paws smashed in fury at the very walls of his ship. Finally, in a brief flash of sanity, he knew that he couldn't face the inevitable fire of atomic disintegrators.

It was a simple thing to create the violent disorganization that freed every drop of id from his vital organs.

They found him lying dead in a little pool of phosphorus.

'Poor kitty,' said Morton. 'I wonder what he thought when

he saw us appear ahead of him, after his own sun disappeared. Knowing nothing of anti-accelerators, he couldn't know that we could stop short in space, whereas it would take him more than three hours to decelerate: and in the meantime he'd be drawing farther and farther away from where he wanted to go. He couldn't know that by stopping, we flashed past him at millions of miles a second. Of course, he didn't have a chance once he left our ship. The whole world must have seemed topsy-turvy.'

'Never mind the sympathy,' he heard Kent say behind him. 'We've got a job – to kill every cat in that miserable world.'

Korita murmured softly: 'That should be simple. They are but primitives; and we have merely to sit down, and they will come to us, cunningly expecting to delude us.'

Smith snapped: 'You fellows make me sick! Kitty was the toughest nut we ever had to crack. He had everything he needed to defeat us –'

Morton smiled as Korita interrupted blandly: 'Exactly, my dear Smith, except that he reacted according to the biological impulses of his type. His defeat was already foreshadowed when we unerringly analyzed him as a criminal from a certain era of his civilization.

'It was history, honorable Mr. Smith, our knowledge of history that defeated him,' said the Japanese archaeologist, reverting to the ancient politeness of his race.

FIREWATER

by William Tenn

The Aliens were destroying humanity's self-respect: the Primeys were giving men wonderful devices, and acute headaches, and – nobody had an answer. But sometimes 'Business As Usual' pays off !

The hairiest, dirtiest and oldest of the three visitors from Arizona scratched his back against the plastic of the webfoam chair. 'Insinuations are lavender nearly,' he remarked by way of opening the conversation.

His two companions – the thin young man with dripping eyes, and the woman whose good looks were marred chiefly by incredibly decayed teeth – giggled and relaxed. The thin young man said 'Gabble, gabble, honk!' under his breath, and the other two nodded emphatically.

Greta Seidenheim looked up from the tiny stenographic machine resting on a pair of the most exciting knees her employer had been able to find in Greater New York. She swiveled her blond beauty at him. 'That too, Mr. Hebster?'

The president of Hebster Securities, Inc., waited until the memory of her voice ceased to tickle his ears: he had much clear thinking to do. Then he nodded and said resonantly, 'That too, Miss Seidenheim. Close phonetic approximations of the gabble-honk and remember to indicate when it sounds like a question and when like an exclamation.'

He rubbed his recently manicured fingernails across the desk drawer containing his fully loaded Parabellum. Check. The communication buttons with which he could summon any quantity of Hebster Securities personnel up to the nine hundred working at present in the Hebster Building lay some inches from the other hand. Check. And there were the doors here, the doors there, behind which his uniformed bodyguard stood poised to burst in at a signal which would blaze before them the moment his right foot came off the tiny spring set in the floor. *And* check.

Algernon Hebster could talk business – even with Primeys.

Courteously, he nodded at each one of his visitors from Arizona; he smiled ruefully at what the dirty shapeless masses they wore on their feet were doing to the calf-deep rug that had been woven specially for his private office. He had greeted them when Miss Seidenheim had escorted them in. They had laughed in his face.

'Suppose we rattle off some introductions. You know me. I'm Hebster, Algernon Hebster – you asked for me specifically at the desk in the lobby. If it's important to the conversation, my secretary's name is Greta Seidenheim. And you, sir?'

He had addressed the old fellow, but the thin young man leaned forward in his seat and held out a taut, almost transparent hand. 'Names?' he inquired. 'Names are round if not revealed. Consider names. How many names? Consider names, *reconsider* names!'

The woman leaned forward too, and the smell from her diseased mouth reached Hebster even across the enormous space of his office. 'Rabble and reaching and all the upward clash,' she intoned, spreading her hands as if in agreement with an obvious point. 'Emptiness derogating itself into infinity –'

'Into duration,' the older man corrected.

'Into infinity,' the woman insisted.

'Gabble, gabble, honk?' the young man queried bitterly.

'Listen!' Hebster roared. 'When I asked for –'

The communicator buzzed and he drew a deep breath and pressed a button. His receptionist's voice boiled out rapidly, fearfully:

'I remember your orders, Mr. Hebster, but those two men from the UM Special Investigating Commission are here again and they look as if they mean business. I mean they look as if they'll make trouble.'

'Yost and Funatti?'

'Yes, sir. From what they said to each other, I think they know you have three Primeys in there. They asked me what are you trying to do – deliberately inflame the Firsters? They said they're going to invoke full supranational powers and force an entry if you don't –'

'Stall them.'

'But, Mr. Hebster, the *UM Special Investigating* –'

'Stall them, I said. Are you a receptionist or a swinging door? Use your imagination, Ruth. You have a nine-hundred-man organization and a ten-million-dollar corporation at your disposal. You can stage any kind of farce in that outer office you want – up to and including the deal where some actor made up to look like me walks in and drops dead at their feet. Stall them and I'll nod a bonus at you. *Stall them.*' He clicked off, looked up.

His visitors, at least, were having a fine time. They had turned to face each other in a reeking triangle of gibberish. Their voices rose and fell argumentatively, pleadingly, decisively; but all Algernon Hebster's ears could register of what they said were very many sounds similar to *gabble* and an occasional, indisputable *honk!*

His lips curled contempt inward. Humanity prime! *These* messes? Then he lit a cigarette and shrugged. Oh, well. Humanity prime. And business is business.

Just remember they're not supermen, he told himself. *They may be dangerous, but they're not supermen. Not by a long shot. Remember that epidemic of influenza that almost wiped them out, and how you diddled those two other Primeys last month. They're not supermen, but they're not humanity either. They're just different.*

He glanced at his secretary and approved. Greta Seidenheim clacked away on her machine as if she were recording the curtest, the tritest of business letters. He wondered what system she was using to catch the intonations. Trust Greta, though, she'd do it.

'Gabble, honk! Gabble, gabble, gabble, honk, honk. Gabble, honk, gabble gabble, honk? Honk.'

What had precipitated all this conversation? He'd only asked for their names. Didn't they use names in Arizona? Surely, they knew that it was customary here. They claimed to know at least as much as he about such matters.

Maybe it was something else that had brought them to New York this time – maybe something about the Aliens? He felt the short hairs rise on the back of his neck and he smoothed them down self consciously.

Trouble was it was so *easy* to learn their language. It was such a very simple matter to be able to understand them in these talkative moments. Almost as easy as falling off a log – or jumping off a cliff.

Well, his time was limited. He didn't know how long Ruth could hold the UM investigators in his outer office. Somehow he had to get a grip on the meeting again without offending them in any of the innumerable, highly dangerous ways in which Primeys could be offended.

He rapped the desk top – gently. The gabble-honk stopped short at the hyphen. The woman rose slowly.

'On this question of names,' Hebster began doggedly, keeping his eyes on the woman, 'since you people claim –'

The woman writhed agonizingly for a moment and sat down on the floor. She smiled at Hebster. With her rotted teeth, the smile had all the brilliance of a dead star.

Hebster cleared his throat and prepared to try again.

'If you want names,' the older man said suddenly, 'you can call me Larry.'

The president of Hebster Securities shook himself and managed to say 'Thanks' in a somewhat weak but not too surprised voice. He looked at the thin young man.

'You can call me Theseus.' The young man looked sad as he said it.

'Theseus? Fine!' One thing about Primeys when you started clicking with them, you really moved along. But *Theseus!* Wasn't that just like a Primey? Now the woman, and they could begin.

They were all looking at the woman, even Greta with a

curiosity which had sneaked up past her beauty-parlor glaze.

'Name,' the woman whispered to herself. 'Name a name.'

Oh, no, Hebster groaned. *Let's not stall here.*

Larry evidently had decided that enough time had been wasted. He made a suggestion to the woman. 'Why not call yourself Moe?'

The young man – Theseus, it was now – also seemed to get interested in the problem. 'Rover's a good name,' he announced helpfully.

'How about Gloria?' Hebster asked desperately.

The woman considered. 'Moe, Rover, Gloria,' she mused. 'Larry, Theseus, Seidenheim, Hebster, me.' She seemed to be running a total.

Anything might come out, Hebster knew. But at least they were not acting snobbish any more: they were talking down on his level now. Not only no gabble-honk, but none of this sneering double-talk which was almost worse. At least they were making sense – of a sort.

'For the purposes of this discussion,' the woman said at last, 'my name will be . . . will be – My name *is* S.S. Lusitania.'

'Fine!' Hebster roared, letting the word he'd kept bubbling on his lips burst out. 'That's a *fine* name. Larry, Theseus and . . . er, S.S. Lusitania. Fine bunch of people. Sound. Let's get down to business. You came here on business, I take it?'

'Right,' Larry said. 'We heard about you from two others who left home a month ago to come to New York. They talked about you when they got back to Arizona.'

'They did, eh? I hoped they would.'

Theseus slid off his chair and squatted next to the woman who was making plucking motions at the air. 'They talked about you,' he repeated. 'They said you treated them very well, that you showed them as much respect as a thing like you could generate. They also said you cheated them.'

'Oh, well, Theseus,' Hebster spread his manicured hands. 'I'm a businessman.'

'You're a businessman,' S.S. Lusitania agreed, getting to her feet stealthily and taking a great swipe with both hands at something invisible in front of her face. 'And here, in this spot, at this moment, so are we. You can have what we've brought, but you'll pay for it. And don't think you can cheat *us*.'

Her hands, cupped over each other, came down to her waist. She pulled them apart suddenly and a tiny eagle fluttered out. It flapped toward the fluorescent panels glowing in the ceiling. Its flight was hampered by the heavy, striped shield upon its breast, by the bunch of arrows it held in one claw, by the olive branch it grasped with the other. It turned its miniature bald head and gasped at Algernon Hebster, then began to drift rapidly down to the rug. Just before it hit the floor, it disappeared.

Hebster shut his eyes, remembering the strip of bunting that had fallen from the eagle's beak when it had turned to gasp. There had been words printed on the bunting, words too small to see at the distance, but he was sure the words would have read '*E Pluribus Unum*.' He was as certain of that as he was of the necessity of acting unconcerned over the whole incident, unconcerned as the Primeys. Professor Kleimbocher said Primeys were mental drunkards. But why did they give everyone else the D.T.'s?

He opened his eyes. 'Well,' he said, 'what have you to sell?'

Silence for a moment. Theseus seemed to forget the point he was trying to make; S.S. Lusitania stared at Larry.

Larry scratched his right side through heavy, stinking cloth.

'Oh, an infallible method for defeating anyone who attempts to apply the *reductio ad absurdum* to a reasonable proposition you advance.' He yawned smugly and began scratching his left side.

Hebster grinned because he was feeling so good. 'No. Can't use it.'

'Can't use it?' The old man was trying hard to look amazed. He shook his head. He stole a sideways glance at S.S. Lusitania.

She smiled again and wriggled to the floor. 'Larry still isn't talking a language you can understand, Mr. Hebster,' she cooed, very much like a fertilizer being friendly. 'We came here with something we know you need badly. Very badly.'

'Yes?' *They're like those two Primeys last month,* Hebster exulted: *they don't know what's good and what isn't. Wonder if their masters would know. Well, and if they did – who does business with Aliens?*

'We . . . have,' she spaced the words carefully, trying pathetically for a dramatic effect, 'a new shade of red, but not merely that. Oh, *no!* A new shade of red, and a full set of color values derived from it! A complete set of color values derived from this one shade of red, Mr. Hebster! Think what a non-objectivist painter can do with such a –'

'Don't sell me, lady. Theseus, do you want to have a go now?'

Theseus had been frowning at the green foundation of the desk. He leaned back, looking satisfied. Hebster realized abruptly that the tension under his right foot had disappeared. Somehow, Theseus had become cognizant of the signal-spring set in the floor; and, somehow, he had removed it.

He had disintegrated it without setting off the alarm to which it was wired.

Giggles from three Primey throats and a rapid exchange of 'gabble-honk.' Then they all knew what Theseus had done and how Hebster had tried to protect himself. They weren't angry, though – and they didn't sound triumphant. Try to understand Primey behavior!

No need to get unduly alarmed – the price of dealing with these characters was a nervous stomach. The rewards, on the other hand –

Abruptly, they were businesslike again.

Theseus snapped out his suggestion with all the finality of a bazaar merchant making his last, absolutely the last offer. 'A set of population indices which can be correlated with –'

'No, Theseus,' Hebster told him gently.

Then, while Hebster sat back and enjoyed, temporarily forgetting the missing coil under his foot, they poured out more, desperately, feverishly, weaving in and out of each other's sentences.

'A portable neutron stabilizer for high altit –'

'More than fifty ways of saying "however" without –'

'. . . So that every housewife can do an *entrechat* while cook –'

'. . . Synthetic fabric with the drape of silk and manufactura –'

'. . . Decorative pattern for bald heads using the follicles as –'

'. . . Complete and utter refutation of all pyramidologists from –'

'All right!' Hebster roared, '*All right !* That's enough!'

Greta Seidenheim almost forgot herself and sighed with relief. Her stenographic machine had been sounding like a centrifuge.

'Now,' said the executive. 'What do you want in exchange?'

'One of those we said is the one you want, eh?' Larry muttered. 'Which one – the pyramidology refutation? That's it, I betcha.'

S.S. Lusitania waved her hands contemptuously. 'Bishop's miters, you fool! The new red color values excited him. The new –'

Ruth's voice came over the communicator. 'Mr. Hebster, Yost and Funatti are back. I stalled them, but I just received word from the lobby receptionist that they're back and on their way upstairs. You have two minutes, maybe three. And they're so mad they almost look like Firster's themselves!'

'Thanks. When they climb out of the elevator, do what you can without getting too illegal.' He turned to his guests. 'Listen –'

They had gone off again.

'Gabble, gabble, honk, honk, honk? Gabble, honk, *gabble*, gabble! Gabble, honk, gabble, honk, gabble, honk, honk.'

Could they honestly make sense out of these throat-clearings and half-sneezes? Was it really a language as superior to all previous languages of man as . . . as the Aliens were supposed to be to man himself? Well, at least they could communicate with the Aliens by means of it. And the Aliens, the Aliens –

He recollected abruptly the two angry representatives of the world state who were hurtling towards his office.

'Listen, friends. You came here to sell. You've shown me your stock, and I've seen something I'd like to buy. *What* exactly is immaterial. The only question now is what you want for it. And let's make it fast. I have some other business to transact.'

The woman with the dental nightmare stamped her foot. A cloud no larger than a man's hand formed near the ceiling, burst and deposited a pailful of water on Hebster's fine custom-made rug.

He ran a manicured forefinger around the inside of his collar so that his bulging neck veins would not burst. Not right now, anyway. He looked at Greta and regained confidence from the serenity with which she waited for more conversation to transcribe. There was a model of business precision for you. The Primeys might pull what one of them had in London two years ago, before they were barred from all metropolitan areas – increased a housefly's size to that of an elephant – and Greta Seidenheim would go on separating fragments of conversation into the appropriate shorthand symbols.

With all their power, why didn't they *take* what they wanted? Why trudge wearisome miles to cities and attempt to smuggle themselves into illegal audiences with operators like Hebster, when most of them were caught easily and sent back to the reservation and those that weren't were cheated unmercifully by the 'straight' humans they encountered? Why didn't they just blast their way in, take their weird and pathetic prizes and toddle back to their masters? For that matter, why didn't their masters – But Primey psych was Primey psych – not for this world, nor of it.

'We'll tell you what we want in exchange,' Larry began in the middle of a honk. He held up a hand on which the length of the fingernails was indicated graphically by the grime beneath them and began to tot up the items, bending a digit for each item. 'First, a hundred paper-bound copies of Melville's "Moby Dick". Then, twenty-five crystal radio sets, with earphones; two earphones for each set. Then, two Empire State Buildings or three Radio Cities, whichever is more convenient.

We want those with foundations intact. A reasonably good copy of the "Hermes" statue by Praxiteles. And an electric toaster, *circa* 1941. That's about all, isn't it, Theseus?'

Theseus bent over until his nose rested against his knees.

Hebster groaned. The list wasn't as bad as he'd expected – remarkable the way their masters always yearned for the electric gadgets and artistic achievements of Earth – but he had so little time to bargain with them. *Two* Empire State Buildings!

'Mr. Hebster,' his receptionist chattered over the communicator. 'Those SIC men – I managed to get a crowd out in the corridor to push toward their elevator when it came to this floor, and I've locked the . . . I mean I'm trying to . . . but I don't think – Can you –'

'Good girl! You're doing fine!'

'Is that all we want, Theseus?' Larry asked again. 'Gabble?'

Hebster heard a crash in the outer office and footsteps running across the floor.

'See here, Mr. Hebster,' Theseus said at last, 'if you don't want to buy Larry's *reductio ad absurdum* exploder, and you don't like my method of decorating bald heads for all its innate artistry, how about a system of musical notation –'

Somebody tried Hebster's door, found it locked. There was a knock on the door, repeated most immediately with more urgency.

'He's *already* found something he wants,' S.S. Lusitania snapped. 'Yes, Larry, that was the complete list.'

Hebster plucked a handful of hair from his already receding forehead. 'Good! Now, look, I can give you everything but the two Empire State Buildings and the three Radio Cities.'

'*Or* the three Radio Cities,' Larry corrected. 'Don't try to cheat us! Two Empire State Buildings *or* three Radio Cities. Whichever is more convenient. Why . . . isn't it worth that to you?'

'Open this door!' a bull-mad voice yelled. 'Open this door in the name of United Mankind!'

'Miss Seidenheim, open the door,' Hebster said loudly and winked at his secretary who rose, stretched and began a thoughtful, slow-motion study in the direction of the locked panel. There was a crash as of a pair of shoulders being thrown against it. Hebster knew that his office door could withstand a medium-sized tank. But there was a limit even to delay when it came to fooling around with the UM Special Investigating Commission. Those boys knew their Primeys and their Primey-dealers; they were empowered to shoot first and ask questions afterwards – as the questions occurred to them.

'It's not a matter of whether it's worth my while,' Hebster told them rapidly as he shepherded them to the exit behind his desk. 'For reasons I'm sure you aren't interested in, I just can't give away two Empire State Buildings and/or three Radio Cities with foundations intact – not at the moment. I'll give you the rest of it, and –'

'Open this door or we start blasting it down!'

'Please, gentlemen, please,' Greta Seidenheim told them sweetly. 'You'll kill a poor working girl who's trying awfully hard to let you in. The lock's stuck.' She fiddled with the doorknob, watching Hebster with a trace of anxiety in her fine eyes.

'And to replace those items,' Hebster was going on. 'I will –'

'What I mean,' Theseus broke in, 'is this. You know the greatest single difficulty composers face in the twelve-tone technique?'

'I can offer you,' the executive continued doggedly, sweat bursting out of his skin like spring freshets, 'complete architectural blueprints of the Empire State Building and Radio City, plus five . . . no, I'll make it ten . . scale models of each. And you get the rest of the stuff you asked for. That's it. Take it or leave it. Fast!'

They glanced at each other, as Hebster threw the exit door open and gestured to the five liveried bodyguards waiting near his private elevator. '*Done*,' they said in unison.

'Good!' Hebster almost squeaked. He pushed them through the doorway and said to the tallest of the five men: 'Nineteenth floor!'

He slammed the exit shut just as Miss Seidenheim opened

the outer office door. Yost and Funatti, in the bottle-green police uniform of the UM, charged through. Without pausing, they ran to where Hebster stood and plucked the exit open. They could all hear the elevator descending.

Funatti, a little, olive-skinned man, sniffed, 'Primeys,' he muttered. 'He had Primeys here, all right. Smell that unwash, Yost?'

'Yeah,' said the bigger man. 'Come on. The emergency stairway. We can track that elevator!'

They holstered their service weapons and clattered down the metal-tipped stairs. Below, the elevator stopped.

Hebster's secretary was at the communicator. 'Maintenance!' She waited. 'Maintenance, automatic locks on the nineteenth floor exit until the party Mr. Hebster just sent down gets to a lab somewhere else. And keep apologizing to those cops until then. Remember, they're SIC.'

'Thanks, Greta,' Hebster said, switching to the personal now that they were alone. He plumped into his desk chair and blew out gustily: 'There must be easier ways of making a million.'

She raised two perfect blond eyebrows. 'Or of being an absolute monarch right inside the parliament of man?'

'If they wait long enough,' he told her lazily, 'I'll *be* the UM, modern global government and all. Another year or two might do it.'

'Aren't you forgetting one Vandermeer Dempsey? His huskies also want to replace the UM. Not to mention their colorful plans for you. And there are an awful, awful lot of them.'

'They don't worry me, Greta. *Humanity First* will dissolve overnight once that decrepit old demagogue gives up the ghost.' He stabbed at the communicator button. 'Maintenance! Maintenance, that party I sent down arrived at a safe lab yet?'

'No, Mr. Hebster. But everything's going all right. We sent them up to the twenty-fourth floor and got the SIC men re-routed downstairs to the personnel levels. Uh, Mr. Hebster – about the SIC. We take your orders and all that, but none of us wants to get in trouble with the Special Investigating Commission. According to the latest laws, it's practically a capital offense to obstruct 'em.'

'Don't worry,' Hebster told him. 'I've never let one of my employees down yet. The boss fixes everything is the motto here. Call me when you've got those Primeys safely hidden and ready for questioning.'

He turned back to Greta. 'Get that stuff typed before you leave and into Professor Kleimbocher's hands. He thinks he may have a new angle on their gabble-honk.'

She nodded. 'I wish you could use recording apparatus instead of making me sit over an old-fashioned click-box.'

'So do I. But Primeys enjoy reaching out and putting a hex on electrical apparatus – when they aren't collecting it for the Aliens. I had a raft of wire and tape recorders busted in the middle of Primey interviews before I decided that human stenos were the only answer. And a Primey may get around to bollixing them some day.'

'Cheerful thought. I must remember to dream about the possibility some cold night. Well, I should complain,' she muttered as she went into her own little office, 'Primey hexes built this business and pay my salary as well as supply me with the sparkling little knicknacks I love so well.'

That was not quite true, Hebster remembered as he sat waiting for the communicator to buzz the news of his recent guests' arrival in a safe lab. Something like ninety-five per cent of Hebster Securities had been built out of Primey gadgetry extracted from them in various fancy deals, but the base of it all had been the small investment bank he had inherited from his father, back in the days of the Half-War – the days when the Aliens had first appeared on Earth.

The fearfully intelligent dots swirling in their variously shaped multicolored bottles were completely outside the pale of human understanding. There had been no way at all to communicate with them for a time.

A humorist had remarked back in those early days that the Aliens came not to bury man, not to conquer or enslave him. They had a truly dreadful mission – to ignore him!

No one knew, even today, what part of the galaxy the Aliens came from. Or why. No one knew what the total of their small visiting population came to. Or how they operated their wide-open and completely silent spaceships. The few things that had been discovered about them on the occasions when they deigned to swoop down and examine some human enterprise, with the aloof amusement of the highly civilized tourist, had served to confirm a technological superiority over Man that strained and tore the capacity of his richest imagination. A sociological treatise Hebster had read recently suggested that they operated from concepts as far in advance of modern science as a meteorologist sowing a drought-struck area with dry ice was beyond the primitive agriculturist blowing a ram's horn at the heavens in a frantic attempt to wake the slumbering gods of rain.

Prolonged, infinitely dangerous observation had revealed, for example, that the dots-in-bottles seemed to have developed past the need for prepared tools of any sort. They worked directly on the material itself, shaping it to need, evidently creating and destroying matter at will!

Some humans had communicated with them –

They didn't stay human.

Men with superb brains had looked into the whirring, flickering settlements established by the outsiders. A few had returned with tales of wonders they had realized dimly and not quite seen. Their descriptions always sounded as if their eyes had been turned off at the most crucial moments or a mental fuse had blown just this side of understanding.

Others – such celebrities as a President of Earth, a three-time winner of the Nobel Prize, famous poets – had evidently broken through the fence somehow. These, however, were the ones who didn't return. They stayed in the Alien settlements in the Gobi, the Sahara, the American Southwest. Barely able to fend for themselves, despite newly acquired and almost un-believable powers, they shambled worshipfully around the out-siders speaking, with weird writhings of larynx and nasal passage, what was evidently a human approximation of their masters' language – a kind of pidgin Alien. Talking with a

Primey, someone had said, was like a blind man trying to read a page of Braille originally written for an octopus.

And that these bearded, bug-ridden, stinking derelicts, these chattering wrecks drunk and sodden on the logic of an entirely different life-form, were the heavy yellow cream of the human race didn't help people's egos any.

Humans and Primeys despised each other almost from the first; humans for Primey subservience and helplessness in human terms, Primeys for human ignorance and ineptness in Alien terms. And, except when operating under Alien orders and through barely legal operators like Hebster, Primeys didn't communicate with humans any more than their masters did.

When institutionalized, they either gabble-honked themselves into an early grave or, losing patience suddenly, they might dissolve a path to freedom right through the walls of the asylum and any attendants who chanced to be in the way. Therefore the enthusiasm of sheriff and deputy, nurse and orderly, had waned considerably and the forcible incarceration of Primeys had almost ceased.

Since the two groups were so far apart psychologically as to make mating between them impossible, the ragged miracle-workers had been honored with the status of a separate classification:

Humanity Prime. Not better than humanity, not necessarily worse – but different, and dangerous.

What made them that way? Hebster rolled his chair back and examined the hole in the floor from which the alarm spring had spiraled. Theseus had disintegrated it – *how?* With a thought? Telekinesis, say, applied to all the molecules of the metal simultaneously, making them move rapidly and at random. Or possibly he had merely moved the spring somewhere else. Where? In space? In hyperspace? In time? Hebster shook his head and pulled himself back to the efficiently smooth and sanely useful desk surface.

'Mr. Hebster?' the communicator inquired abruptly, and he jumped a bit, 'this is Margritt of General Lab 23B. Your Primeys just arrived. Regular check?'

Regular check meant drawing them out on every conceivable technical subject by the nine specialists in the general laboratory. This involved firing questions at them with the rapidity of a police interrogation, getting them off balance and keeping them there in the hope that a useful and unexpected bit of scientific knowledge would drop.

'Yes,' Hebster told him. 'Regular check. But first let a textile man have a whack at them. In fact let him take charge of the check.'

A pause. 'The only textile man in this section is Charlie Verus.'

'Well?' Hebster asked in mild irritation. 'Why put it like that? He's competent I hope. What does personnel say about him?'

'Personnel says he's competent.'

'Then there you are. Look, Margritt, I have the SIC running around my building with blood in its enormous eye. I don't have time to muse over your departmental feuds. Put Verus on.'

'Yes, Mr. Hebster. Hey Bert! Get Charlie Verus. Him.'

Hebster shook his head and chuckled. These technicians! Verus was probably brilliant and nasty.

The box crackled again: 'Mr. Hebster? Mr. Verus.' The voice expressed boredom to the point of obvious affectation. But the man was probably good despite his neuroses. Hebster Securities, Inc., had a first-rate personnel department.

'Verus? Those Primeys, I want you to take charge of the check. One of them knows how to make a synthetic fabric with the drape of silk. Get that first and then go after anything else they have.'

'Primeys, Mr. Hebster?'

'I said Primeys, Mr. Verus. You are a textile technician, please to remember, and not the straight or ping-pong half of a comedy routine. Get humping. I want a report on that synthetic fabric by tomorrow. Work all night if you have to.'

'Before we do, Mr. Hebster, you might be interested in a small piece of information. There is *already* in existence a synthetic which falls better than silk –'

114

'I know,' his employer told him shortly. 'Cellulose acetate. Unfortunately, it has a few disadvantages: low melting-point, tends to crack; separate and somewhat inferior dyestuffs have to be used for it; poor chemical resistance. Am I right?'

There was no immediate answer, but Hebster could feel the dazed nod. He went on. 'Now, we also have protein fibers. They dye well and fall well, have the thermoconductivity control necessary for wearing apparel, but don't have the tensile strength of synthetic fabrics. An *artificial* protein fiber might be the answer: it would drape as well as silk, might be we could use the acid dyestuffs we use on silk which result in shades that dazzle female customers and cause them to fling wide their pocketbooks. There are a lot of *ifs* in that, I know, but one of those Primeys said something about a synthetic with the drape of silk, and I don't think he'd be sane enough to be referring to cellulose acetate. Nor nylon, orlon, vinyl chloride, or anything else we already have and use.'

'You've looked into textile problems, Mr. Hebster.'

'I have. I've looked into everything to which there are big gobs of money attached. And now suppose you go look into those Primeys. Several million women are waiting breathlessly for the secrets concealed in their beards. Do you think, Verus, that with the personal and scientific background I've just given you it's possible you might now get around to doing the job you are paid to do?'

'Um-m-m. Yes.'

Hebster walked to the office closet and got his hat and coat. He liked working under pressure; he liked to see people jump up straight whenever he barked. And now, he liked the prospect of relaxing.

He grimaced at the webfoam chair that Larry had used. No point in having it resquirted. Have a new one made.

'I'll be at the University,' he told Ruth on his way out. 'You can reach me through Professor Kleimbocher. But don't, unless it's very important. He gets unpleasantly annoyed when he's interrupted.'

She nodded. Then, very hesitantly: 'Those two men – Yost

and Funatti – from the Special Investigating Commission? They said no one would be allowed to leave the building.'

'Did they now?' he chuckled. 'I think they were angry. They've been that way before. But unless and until they can hang something on me – And Ruth, tell my bodyguard to go home, except for the man with the Primeys. He's to check with me, wherever I am, every two hours.'

He ambled out, being careful to smile benevolently at every third executive and fifth typist in the large office. A private elevator and entrance was all very well for an occasional crisis, but Hebster liked to taste his successes in as much public as possible.

It would be good to see Kleimbocher again. He had a good deal of faith in the linguistic approach; grants from his corporation had tripled the size of the university's philology department. After all, the basic problem between man and Primey as well as man and Alien was one of communication. Any attempt to learn their science, to adjust their mental processes and logic into safer human channels, would have to be preceded by understanding.

It was up to Kleimbocher to find that understanding, not him. 'I'm Hebster,' he thought. 'I *employ* the people who solve problems. And then I make money off them.'

Somebody got in front of him. Somebody else took his arm. 'I'm Hebster,' he repeated automatically, but out loud. '*Algernon* Hebster.'

'Exactly the Hebster we want,' Funatti said holding tightly on to his arm. 'You don't mind coming along with us?'

'Is this an arrest?' Hebster asked the larger Yost who now moved aside to let him pass. Yost was touching his holstered weapon with dancing fingertips.

The SIC man shrugged. 'Why ask such questions?' he countered. 'Just come along and be sociable, kind of. People want to talk to you.'

He allowed himself to be dragged through the lobby ornate with murals by radical painters and nodded appreciation at the doorman who, staring right through his captors, said enthusiastically, 'Good *afternoon*, Mr. Hebster.' He made himself fairly comfortable on the back seat of the dark-green SIC car, a late model Hebster Monowheel.

'Surprised to see you minus your bodyguard,' Yost, who was driving, remarked over his shoulder.

'Oh, I gave them the day off.'

'As soon as you were through with the Primeys? No,' Funatti admitted, 'we never did find out where you cached them. That's one big building you own, mister. And the UM Special Investigating Commission is notoriously understaffed.'

'Not forgetting it's also notoriously underpaid,' Yost broke in.

'I couldn't forget that if I tried,' Funatti assured him. 'You know, Mr. Hebster, I wouldn't have sent my bodyguard off if I'd been in your shoes. Right now there's something about five times as dangerous as Primeys after you. I mean Humanity Firsters.'

'Vandermeer Dempsey's crackpots? Thanks, but I think I'll survive.'

'That's all right. Just don't give any long odds on the proposition. Those people have been expanding fast and furious. *The Evening Humanitarian* alone has a tremendous circulation. And when you figure their weekly newspapers, their penny booklets and throwaway handbills, it adds up to an impressive amount of propaganda. Day after day they bang away editorially at the people who're making money off the Aliens and Primeys. Of course, they're really hitting at the UM, like always, but if an ordinary Firster met you on the street, he'd be as likely to cut your heart out as not. Not interested? Sorry. Well, maybe you'll like this. *The Evening Humanitarian* has a cute name for you.'

Yost guffawed. 'Tell him, Funatti.'

The corporation president looked at the little man inquiringly.

'They call you,' Funatti said with great savoring deliberation, 'they call you an interplanetary pimp!'

Emerging at last from the crosstown underpass, they sped up the very latest addition to the strangling city's facilities – the

East Side Air-Floating Super-Duper Highway, known familiarly as Dive-Bomber Drive. At the Forty-Second Street offway, the busiest road exit in Manhattan, Yost failed to make a traffic signal. He cursed absent-mindedly and Hebster found himself nodding the involuntary passenger's agreement. They watched the elevator section dwindling downward as the cars that were to mount the highway spiraled up from the right. Between the two, there rose and fell the steady platforms of harbor traffic while, stacked like so many decks of cards, the pedestrian stages awaited their turn below.

'Look! Up there, straight ahead! See it?'

Hebster and Funatti followed Yost's long, waggling forefinger with their eyes. Two hundred feet north of the offway and almost a quarter of a mile straight up, a brown object hung in obvious fascination. Every once in a while a brilliant blue dot would enliven the heavy murk imprisoned in its bell-jar shape only to twirl around the side and be replaced by another.

'Eyes? You think they're eyes?' Funatti asked, rubbing his small dark fists against each other futilely. 'I know what the scientists say – that every dot is equivalent to one person and the whole bottle is like a family or a city, maybe. But how do they know? It's a theory, a guess. *I* say they're eyes.'

Yost hunched his great body half out of the open window and shaded his vision with his uniform cap against the sun. 'Look at it,' they heard him say, over his shoulder. A nasal twang, long-buried, came back into his voice as heaving emotion shook out its cultivated accents. 'A-setting up there, a-staring and a-staring. So all-fired interested in how we get on and off a busy highway! Won't pay us no never mind when we try to talk to it, when we try to find out what it wants, where it comes from, who it is. Oh, no! It's too superior to talk to the likes of us! But it can watch us, hours on end, days without end, light and dark, winter and summer; it can watch us going about our business; and every time we dumb two-legged animals try to do something *we* find complicated, along comes a blasted "dots-in-bottle" to watch and sneer and –'

'Hey there, man,' Funatti leaned forward and tugged at his partner's green jerkin. 'Easy! We're SIC, on business.'

'All the same,' Yost grunted wistfully, as he plopped back into his seat and pressed the power button, 'I wish I had Daddy's little old M-1 Garand right now.' They bowled forward, smoothed into the next long elevator section and started to descend. 'It would be worth the risk of getting *pinged*.'

And this was a UM man, Hebster reflected with acute discomfort. Not only UM, at that, but member of a special group carefully screened for their lack of anti-Primey prejudice, sworn to enforce the reservation laws without discrimination and dedicated to the proposition that Man could somehow achieve equality with Alien.

Well, how much dirt-eating could people do ? People without a business sense, that is. His father had hauled himself out of the pick-and-shovel brigade hand over hand and raised his only son to maneuver always for greater control, to search always for that extra percentage of profit.

But others seemed to have no such abiding interest. Algernon Hebster knew regretfully.

They found it impossible to live with achievements so abruptly made inconsequential by the Aliens. To know with certainty that the most brilliant strokes of which they were capable, the most intricate designs and clever careful workmanship, could be duplicated – and surpassed – in an instant's creation by the outsiders and was of interest to them only as a collector's item. The feeling of inferiority is horrible enough when imagined; but when it isn't feeling but *knowledge*, when it is inescapable and thoroughly demonstrable, covering every aspect of constructive activity, it becomes unbearable and maddening.

No wonder men went berserk under hours of unwinking Alien scrutiny – watching them as they marched in a colorfully uniformed lodge parade, or fished through a hole in the ice, as they painfully maneuvered a giant transcontinental jet to a noiseless landing or sat in sweating, serried rows chanting to a single, sweating man to 'knock it out of the park and sew the whole thing up!' No wonder they seized rusty shotgun or gleaming rifle and sped shot after vindictive shot into a sky poisoned by the contemptuous curiosity of a brown, yellow or vermilion 'bottle.'

Not that it made very much difference. It did give a certain release to nerves backed into horrible psychic corners. But the Aliens didn't notice, and that was most important. The Aliens went right on watching, as if all this shooting and uproar, all these imprecations and weapon-wavings, were all part of the self-same absorbing show they had paid to witness and were determined to see through if for nothing else than the occasional amusing fluff some member of the inexperienced cast might commit.

The Aliens weren't injured, and the Aliens didn't feel attacked. Bullets, shells, buckshot, arrows, pebbles from a slingshot – all Man's miscellany of anger passed through them like the patient and eternal rain coming in the opposite direction. Yet the Aliens had solidity somewhere in their strange bodies. One could judge that by the way they intercepted light and heat. And also –

Also by the occasional *ping*.

Every once in a while, someone would evidently have hurt an Alien slightly. Or more probably just annoyed it by some unknown concomitant of rifle-firing or javelin-throwing.

There would be the barest suspicion of a sound – as if a guitarist had lunged at a string with his fingertip and decided against it one motor impulse too late. And, after this delicate and hardly heard *ping*, quite unspectacularly, the rifleman would be weaponless. He would be standing there sighting stupidly up along his empty curled fingers, elbow cocked out and shoulder hunched in, like a large oafish child who had forgotten when to end the game. Neither his rifle nor a fragment of it would ever be found. And – gravely, curiously, intently – the Alien would go on watching.

The *ping* seemed to be aimed chiefly at weapons. Thus, occasionally, a 155 mm. howitzer was *pinged*, and, also occasionally, unexpectedly, it might be a muscular arm, curving back with another stone, that would disappear to the accompaniment of a tiny elfin note. And yet sometimes – could it be that the Alien, losing interest, had become careless in its irritation? – the entire man, murderously violent and shrieking, would *ping* and be no more.

It was not as if a counter-weapon were being used, but a thoroughly higher order of reply, such as a slap to an insect bite. Hebster, shivering, recalled the time he had seen a black tubular Alien swirl its amber dots over a new substreet excavation, seemingly entranced by the spectacle of men scrabbling at the earth beneath them.

A red-headed Sequoia of Irish labor had looked up from Manhattan's stubborn granite just long enough to shake the sweat from his eyelids. So doing, he had caught sight of the dot-pulsing observer and paused to snarl and lift his pneumatic drill, rattling it in noisy, if functionless, bravado at the sky. He had hardly been noticed by his mates, when the long, dark, speckled representative of a race beyond the stars turned end over end once and *ping*ed.

The heavy drill remained upright for a moment, then dropped as if it had abruptly realized its master was gone. Gone? Almost, he had never been. So thorough had his disappearance been, so rapid, with so little flicker had he been snuffed out – harming and taking with him nothing else – that it had amounted to an act of gigantic and positive noncreation.

No, Hebster decided, making threatening gestures at the Aliens was suicidal. Worse, like everything else that had been tried to date, it was useless. On the other hand, wasn't the *Humanity First* approach a complete neurosis? What *could* you do?

He reached into his soul for an article of fundamental faith, found it. 'I can make money,' he quoted to himself. 'That's what I'm good for. That's what I can always do.'

As they spun to a stop before the dumpy, brown-brick armory that the SIC had appropriated for its own use, he had a shock. Across the street was a small cigar store, the only one on the block. Brand names which had decorated the plate-glass window in all the colors of the copyright had been supplanted recently by great gilt slogans. Familiar slogans they were by now – but this close to a UM office, the Special Investigating

Commission itself?

At the top of the window, the proprietor announced his affiliation in two huge words that almost screamed their hatred across the street:

HUMANITY FIRST!

Underneath these, in the exact center of the window, was the large golden initial of the organization, the wedded letters HF arising out of the huge, symbolic safety razor.

And under that, in straggling script, the theme repeated, reworded and sloganized:

'*Humanity first, last and all the time!*'

The upper part of the door began to get nasty:

'*Deport the Aliens! Send them back to wherever they came from!*'

And the bottom of the door made the store-front's only concession to business:

'*Shop here! Shop Humanitarian!*'

'*Humanitarian!*' Funatti nodded bitterly beside Hebster. 'Ever see what's left of a Primey if a bunch of Firsters catch him without IC protection? Just about enough to pick up with a blotter. I don't imagine you're too happy about boycottshops like that?'

Hebster managed a chuckle as they walked past the saluting, green-uniformed guards. 'There aren't very many Primeyinspired gadgets having to do with tobacco. And if there were, one *Shop Humanitarian* outfit isn't going to break me.'

But it is, he told himself disconsolately. It is going to break me – if it means what it seems to. Organization membership is one thing and so is planetary patriotism, but business is something else.

Hebster's lips moved slowly, in half-remembered catechism: Whatever the proprietor believes in or does not believe in, he has to make a certain amount of money out of that place if he's going to keep the door free of bailiff stickers. He can't do it if he offends the greater part of his possible clientele.

Therefore, since he's still in business and, from all outward signs, doing quite well, it's obvious that he doesn't have to depend on across-the-street UM personnel. Therefore, there must be a fairly substantial trade to offset this among entirely transient customers who not only don't object to his Firstism but are willing to forego the interesting new gimmicks and lower prices in standard items that Primey technology is giving us.

Therefore, it is entirely possible – from this one extremely random but highly significant sample – that the newspapers I read have been lying and the socio-economists I employ are incompetent. It is entirely possible that the buying public, the only aspect of the public in which I have the slightest interest, is beginning a shift in general viewpoint which will profoundly affect its purchasing orientation.

It is possible that the entire UM economy is now at the top of a long slide into Humanity First domination, the secure zone of fanatic blindness demarcated by men like Vandermeer Dempsey. The highly usurious, commercially speculative economy of Imperial Rome made a similar transition in the much slower historical pace of two millennia ago and became, in three brief centuries, a static unbusinesslike world in which banking was a sin and wealth which had not been inherited was gross and dishonorable.

Meanwhile, people may already have begun to judge manufactured items on the basis of morality instead of usability, Hebster realized, as dim mental notes took their stolid place beside forming conclusions. He remembered a folderful of brilliant explanation Market Research had sent up last week dealing with unexpected consumer resistance to the new Evvakleen dishware. He had dismissed the pages of carefully developed thesis – to the effect that women were unconsciously associating the product's name with a certain Katherine Evvakios who had recently made the front page of every tabloid in the world by dint of some fast work with a breadknife on the throats of her five children and two lovers – with a yawning smile after examining its first brightly colored chart.

'Probably nothing more than normal housewifely suspicion

of a radically new idea,' he had muttered, 'after washing dishes for years, to be told it's no longer necessary! She can't believe her Evvakleen dish is still the same after stripping the outermost film of molecules after a meal. Have to hit that educational angle a bit harder – maybe tie it in with the expendable molecules lost by the skin during a shower.'

He'd pencilled a few notes on the margin and flipped the whole problem onto the restless lap of Advertising and Promotion.

But then there had been the seasonal slump in furniture – about a month ahead of schedule. The surprising lack of interest in the Hebster Chubbichair, an item which should have revolutionized men's sitting habits.

Abruptly, he could remember almost a dozen unaccountable disturbances in the market recently, and all in consumer goods. That fits, he decided; any change in buying habits wouldn't be reflected in heavy industry for at least a year. The machine tools plants would feel it before the steel mills; the mills before the smelting and refining combines; and the banks and big investment houses would be the last of the dominoes to topple.

With its capital so thoroughly tied up in research and new production, his business wouldn't survive even a temporary shift of this type. Hebster Securities, Inc. could go like a speck of lint being blown off a coat collar.

Which is a long way to travel from a simple little cigar store. Funatti's jitters about growing Firstist sentiment are contagious! he thought.

If only Kleimbocher could crack the communication problem! If we could talk to the Aliens, find some sort of place for ourselves in their universe. The Firsters would be left without a single political leg!

Hebster realized they were in a large, untidy, map-spattered office and that his escort was saluting a huge, even more untidy man who waved their hands down impatiently and nodded them out of the door. He motioned Hebster to a choice of seats. This consisted of several long walnut-stained benches scattered about the room.

P. Braganza, said the desk nameplate with ornate Gothic flow. P. Braganza had a long, twirlable and tremendously thick mustache. Also, P. Braganza needed a haircut badly. It was as if he and everything in the room had been carefully designed to give the maximum affront to Humanity Firsters. Which, considering their crew-cut, closely shaven, 'Cleanliness is next to Manliness' philosophy, meant that there was a lot of gratuitous unpleasantness in this office when a raid on a street demonstration filled it with jostling fanatics, antiseptically clean and dressed with bare-bone simplicity and neatness.

'So you're worrying about Firster effect on business?'

Hebster looked up, startled.

'No, I don't read your mind,' Braganza laughed through tobacco-stained teeth. He gestured at the window behind his desk. 'I saw you jump just the littlest bit when you noticed that cigar store. And then you stared at it for two full minutes. I knew what you were thinking about.'

'Extremely perceptive of you,' Hebster remarked dryly.

The SIC official shook his head in a violent negative. 'No, it wasn't. It wasn't a bit perceptive. I knew what you were thinking about because I sit up here day after day staring at that cigar store and thinking exactly the same thing. Braganza, I tell myself, that's the end of your job. That's the end of scientific world government. Right there on that cigar-store window.'

He glowered at his completely littered desk top for a moment. Hebster's instincts woke up – there was a sales talk in the wind. He realized the man was engaged in the unaccustomed exercise of looking for a conversational gambit. He felt an itch of fear crawl up his intestines. Why should the SIC, whose power was almost above law and certainly above governments, be trying to dicker with him?

Considering his reputation for asking questions with the snarling end of a rubber hose, Braganza was being entirely too gentle, too talkative, too friendly. Hebster felt like a trapped mouse into whose disconcerted ear a cat was beginning to pour complaints about the dog upstairs.

'Hebster, tell me something. What are your goals?'

'I beg your pardon?'

'What do you want out of life? What do you spend your days planning for, your nights dreaming about? Yost likes the girls and wants more of them. Funatti's a family man, five kids. He's happy in his work because his job's fairly secure, and there are all kinds of pensions and insurance policies to back up his life.'

Braganza lowered his powerful head and began a slow, reluctant pacing in front of the desk.

'Now, I'm a little different. Not that I mind being a glorified cop. I appreciate the regularity with which the finance office pays my salary, of course; and there are very few women in this town who can say that I have received an offer of affection from them with outright scorn. But the one thing for which I would lay down my life is United Mankind. *Would* lay down my life? In terms of blood pressure and heart strain you might say I've already done it! Braganza, I tell myself, you're a lucky dope. You're working for the first world government in human history. Make it count.'

He stopped and spread his arms in front of Hebster. His unbuttoned green jerkin came apart awkwardly and exposed the black slab of hair on his chest. 'That's me. That's basically all there is to Braganza. Now if we're to talk sensibly I have to know as much about you. I ask – what are your goals?'

The President of Hebster Securities, Inc., wet his lips. 'I'm afraid I'm even less complicated.'

'That's all right,' the other man encouraged. 'Put it any way you like.'

'You might say that before everything else I am a businessman. I am interested chiefly in becoming a better businessman, which is to say a bigger one. In other words, I want to be richer than I am.'

Braganza peered at him intently. 'And that's all?'

'All? Haven't you ever heard it said that money isn't everything, but that what it isn't it can buy?'

'It can't buy me.'

Hebster examined him coolly. 'I don't know if you're a

126

sufficiently desirable commodity. I buy what I need, only occasionally making an exception to please myself.'

'I don't like you.' Braganza's voice had become thick and ugly. 'I never liked your kind and there's no sense being polite. I might as well stop trying. I tell you straight out – I think your guts stink.'

Hebster rose. 'In that case, I believe I should thank you for –'

'Sit *down!* You were asked here for a reason. I don't see any point to it, but we'll go through the motions. Sit down.'

Hebster sat. He wondered idly if Braganza received half the salary he paid Greta Seidenheim. Of course, Greta was talented in many different ways and performed several distinct and separately useful services. No, after tax and pension deductions, Braganza was probably fortunate to receive one third of Greta's salary.

He noticed that a newspaper was being proffered him. He took it. Braganza grunted, clumped back behind his desk and swung his swivel chair around to face the window.

It was a week-old copy of *The Evening Humanitarian*. The paper had lost the 'voice-of-a-small-but-highly-articulate-minority' look, Hebster remembered from his last reading of it, and acquired the feel of publishing big business. Even if you cut in half the circulation claimed by the box in the upper left-hand corner, that still gave them three million paying readers.

In the upper right-hand corner, a red-bordered box exhorted the faithful to '*Read Humanitarian!*' A green streamer across the top of the first page announced that '*Making sense is human – to gibber, Prime!*'

But the important item was in the middle of the page. A cartoon.

Half-a-dozen Primeys wearing long, curved beards and insane, tongue-lolling grins, sat in a rickety wagon. They held reins attached to a group of straining and portly gentlemen dressed – somewhat simply – in high silk hats. The fattest and ugliest of these, the one in the lead, had a bit between his teeth. The bit was labeled '*crazy-money*' and the man, 'Algernon Hebster.'

Crushed and splintering under the wheels of the wagon were such varied items as a 'Home Sweet Home' framed motto with a piece of wall attached, a clean-cut youngster in a Boy Scout uniform, a streamlined locomotive and a gorgeous young woman with a squalling infant under each arm.

The caption inquired starkly: 'Lords of Creation – Or Serfs?'

'This paper seems to have developed into a fairly filthy scandal sheet,' Hebster mused out loud. 'I shouldn't be surprised if it makes money.'

'I take it then,' Braganza asked without turning around from his contemplation of the street, 'that you haven't read it very regularly in recent months?'

'I am happy to say I have not.'

'That was a mistake.'

Hebster stared at the clumped locks of black hair. 'Why?' he asked carefully.

'Because it *has* developed into a thoroughly filthy and extremely successful scandal sheet. You're its chief scandal.' Braganza laughed. 'You see these people look upon Primey dealing as more of a sin than a crime. And, according to that morality, you're close to Old Nick himself!'

Shutting his eyes for a moment, Hebster tried to understand people who imagined such a soul-satisfying and beautiful concept as profit to be a thing of dirt and crawling maggots. He sighed. 'I've thought of Firstism as a religion myself.'

That seemed to get the SIC man. He swung around excitedly and pointed with both forefingers. 'I tell you that you are right! It crosses all boundaries – incompatible and warring creeds are absorbed into it. It is willful, witless denial of a highly painful fact – that there are intellects abroad in the universe which are superior to our own. And the denial grows in strength every day that we are unable to contact the Aliens. If, as seems obvious, there is no respectable place for humanity in this galactic civilization, why, say men like Vandermeer Dempsey, then let us preserve our self-conceit at the least. Let's stay close to and revel in the things that are undeniably human. In a few decades, the entire human race will have been sucked into this blinkered vacuum.'

He rose and walked around the desk again. His voice had assumed a terribly earnest, tragically pleading quality. His eyes roved Hebster's face as if searching for a pin-point of weakness, an especially thin spot in the frozen calm.

'Think of it,' he asked Hebster. 'Periodic slaughters of scientists and artists who, in the judgment of Dempsey, have pushed out too far from the conventional center of so-called humanness. An occasional *auto-da-fé* in honor of a merchant caught selling Primey goods –'

'I shouldn't like that,' Hebster admitted, smiling. He thought a moment. 'I see the connection you're trying to establish with the cartoon in *The Evening Humanitarian*.'

'Mister, I shouldn't have to. They want your head on the top of a long stick. They want it because you've become a symbol of dealing successfully for your own ends, with these stellar foreigners, or at least their human errand-boys and chamber-maids. They figure that maybe they can put a stop to Primey-dealing generally if they put a bloody stop to you. And I tell you this – maybe they are right.'

'What exactly do you propose?' Hebster asked in a low voice.

'That you come in with us. We'll make an honest man of you – officially. We want you directing our investigation; except that the goal will not be an extra buck but all-important interracial communication and eventual interstellar negotiation.'

The president of Hebster Securities, Inc. gave himself a few minutes on that one. He wanted to work out a careful reply. And he wanted time – above all, he wanted time!

He was so close to a well-integrated and world-wide commercial empire! For ten years, he had been carefully fitting the component industrial kingdoms into place, establishing suzerainty in this production network and squeezing a little more control out of that economic satrapy. He had found delectable tidbits of power in the dissolution of his civiliza-tion, endless opportunities for wealth in the shards of his race's self-esteem. He required a bare twelve months now to consolidate and co-ordinate. And suddenly – with the open-mouthed shock of a Jim Fiske who had cornered gold on the Exchange only to have the United States Treasury defeat him by releasing enormous quantities from the Government's own hoard – suddenly, Hebster realized he wasn't going to have the time. He was too experienced a player not to sense that a new factor was coming into the game, something outside his tables of actuarial figures, his market graphs and cargo loading indices.

His mouth was clogged with the heavy nausea of unexpected defeat. He forced himself to answer:

'I'm flattered. Braganza, I *really* am flattered. I see that Dempsey has linked us – we stand or fall together. But – I've always been a loner. With whatever help I can buy, I take care of myself. I'm not interested in any goal but the extra buck. First and last, I'm a businessman.'

'Oh, stop it!' The dark man took a turn up and down the office angrily. 'This is a planet-wide emergency. There are times when you can't be a businessman.'

'I deny that. I can't conceive of such a time.'

Braganza snorted. 'You can't be a businessman if you're strapped to a huge pile of blazing faggots. You can't be a businessman if people's minds are so thoroughly controlled that they'll stop eating at their leader's command. You can't be a businessman, my slavering, acquisitive friend, if demand is so well in hand that it ceases to exist.'

'That's impossible!' Hebster had leaped to his feet. To his amazement, he heard his voice climbing up the scale to hysteria. 'There's *always* demand. Always! The trick is to find what new form it's taken and then fill it!'

'Sorry! I didn't mean to make fun of your religion.'

Hebster drew a deep breath and sat down with infinite care. He could almost feel his red corpuscles simmering.

Take it easy, he warned himself, take it easy! This is a man who must be won, not antagonized. They're changing the rules of the market, Hebster, and you'll need every friend you can buy.

Money won't work with this fellow. But there are *other* values –

'Listen to me, Braganza. We're up against the psycho-social consequences of an extremely advanced civilization hitting a comparatively barbarous one. Are you familiar with Professor Kleimbocher's Firewater Theory?'

'That the Alien's logic hits us mentally in the same way as whisky hit the North American Indian? And the Primeys, representing our finest minds, are the equivalent of those Indians who had the most sympathy with the white man's civilization? Yes. It's a strong analogy. Even carried to the Indians who, lying sodden with liquor in the streets of frontier towns, helped create the illusion of the treacherous, lazy, kill-you-for-a-drink aborigines while being so thoroughly despised by their tribesmen that they didn't dare go home for fear of having their throats cut. I've always felt –'

'The only part of that I want to talk about,' Hebster interrupted, 'is the firewater concept. Back in the Indian villages, an ever-increasing majority became convinced that fire-water and gluttonous paleface civilization were synonymous, that they must rise and retake their land forcibly, killing in the process as many drunken renegades as they came across. This group can be equated with Humanity Firsters. Then there was a minority who recognized the white man's superiority in numbers and weapons, and desperately tried to find a way of coming to terms with his civilization – terms that would not include his booze. For them read the UM. Finally, there was my kind of Indian.'

Braganza knitted voluminous eyebrows and hitched himself up to a corner of the desk. 'Hah?' he inquired. 'What kind of Indian were *you*, Hebster?'

'The kind who had enough sense to know that the paleface had not the slightest interest in saving him from slow and painful cultural anemia. The kind of Indian, also, whose instincts were sufficiently sound so that he was scared to death of innovations like firewater and wouldn't touch the stuff to save himself from snake bite. But the kind of Indian –'

'Yes? Go on!'

'The kind who was fascinated by the strange transparent container in which the firewater came! Think how covetous an Indian potter might be of the whisky bottle, something which was completely outside the capacity of his painfully acquired technology. Can't you see him hating, despising and terribly afraid of the smelly amber fluid, which toppled the most stalwart warriors, yet wistful to possess a bottle minus contents? That's about where I see myself, Braganza – the Indian whose greedy curiosity shines through the murk of hysterical clan politics and outsiders' contempt like a lambent flame. I want the new kind of container somehow separated from the firewater.'

Unblinkingly, the great dark eyes stared at his face. A hand came up and smoothed each side of the arched mustachio with long, unknowing twirls. Minutes passed.

'Well, Hebster as our civilization's noble savage,' the SIC man chuckled at last, 'it almost feels right. But what does it mean in terms of the overall problem?'

'I've told you,' Hebster said wearily, hitting the arm of the bench with his open hand, 'that I haven't the slightest interest in the overall problem.'

'And you only want the bottle. I heard you. But you're not a potter, Hebster – you haven't an elementary particle of craftsman's curiosity. All of that historical romance you spout – you don't care if your world drowns in its own agonized juice. You just want a profit.'

'I never claimed an altruistic reason. I leave the general solution to men whose minds are good enough to juggle its complexities – like Kleimbocher.'

'Think somebody like Kleimbocher could do it?'

'I'm almost certain he will. That was our mistake from the beginning – trying to break through with historians and psychologists. Either they've become limited by the study of human societies or – well, this is personal, but I've always felt that the science of the mind attracts chiefly those who've already experienced grave psychological difficulty. While they might achieve such an understanding of themselves in the course of their work as to become better adjusted eventually than individuals who had less problems to begin with, I'd still consider them too essentially unstable for such an intrinsically shocking experience as establishing *rapport* with an Alien. Their internal dynamics inevitably make Primeys of them.'

Braganza sucked at a tooth and considered the wall behind Hebster. 'And all this, you feel, wouldn't apply to Kleimbocher?'

'No, not a philology professor. He has no interest, no intellectual roots in personal and group instability. Kleimbocher's a comparative linguist – a technician, really – a specialist in basic communication. I've been out to the university and watched him work. His approach to the problem is entirely in terms of his subject – communicating with the Aliens instead of trying to understand them. There's been entirely too much intricate speculation about Alien consciousness, sexual attitudes and social organization, about stuff from which we will derive no tangible and immediate good. Kleimbocher's completely pragmatic.'

'All right. I follow you. Only he went Prime this morning.'

Hebster paused, a sentence dangling from his dropped jaw. 'Professor Kleimbocher? *Rudolf* Kleimbocher?' he asked idiotically. 'But he was so close . . . he almost had it . . . an elementary signal dictionary . . . he was about to –'

'He *did*. About nine forty-five. He'd been up all night with a Primey one of the psych professors had managed to hypnotize and gone home unusually optimistic. In the middle of his first class this morning, he interrupted himself in a lecture on medieval cyrillic to . . . to gabble-honk. He sneezed and wheezed at the students for about ten minutes in the usual Primey pattern of initial irritation, then, abruptly giving them up as hopeless, worthless idiots, he levitated himself in that eerie way they almost always do at first. Banged his head against the ceiling and knocked himself out. I don't know what it was, fright, excitement, respect for the old boy perhaps, but the students neglected to tie him up before going for help. By the time they'd come back with the campus SIC man,

Kleimbocher had revived and dissolved one wall of the Graduate School to get out. Here's a snapshot of him about five hundred feet in the air, lying on his back with his arms crossed behind his head, skimming west at twenty miles an hour.'

The executive studied the little paper rectangle with blinking eyes. 'You radioed the air force to chase him, of course.'

'What's the use? We've been through *that* enough times. He'd either increase his speed and generate a tornado, drop like a stone and get himself smeared all over the countryside or materialize stuff like wet coffee grounds and gold ingots inside the jets of the pursuing plane. Nobody's caught a Primey yet in the first flush of . . . whatever they do feel at first. And we might stand to lose anything from a fairly expensive hunk of aircraft, including pilot, to a couple of hundred acres of New Jersey topsoil.'

Hebster groaned. 'But the eighteen years of research that he represented!'

'Yeah. That's where we stand. Blind Alley umpteen hundred thousand or thereabouts. Whatever the figure is, it's awfully close to the end. If you can't crack the Alien on a straight linguistic basis, you can't crack the Alien at all, period, end of paragraph. Our most powerful weapons affect them like bubble pipes, and our finest minds are good for nothing better than to serve them in low, fawning idiocy. But the Primeys are all that's left. We might be able to talk sense to the Man if not the Master.'

'Except that Primeys, by definition, don't talk sense.'

Braganza nodded. 'But since they were human – *ordinary* human – to start with, they represent a hope. We always knew we might some day have to fall back on our only real contact. That's why the Primey protective laws are so rigid; why the Primey reservation compounds surrounding Alien settlements are guarded by our military detachments. The lynch spirit has been evolving into the pogrom spirit as human resentment and discomfort have been growing. Humanity First is beginning to feel strong enough to challenge United Mankind. And honestly,

134

Hebster, at this point neither of us know which would survive a real fight. But you're one of the few who have talked to Primeys, worked with them –'

'Just on business.'

'Frankly, that much of a start is a thousand times further along than the best that we've been able to manage. It's so blasted ironical that the only people who've had any conversation at all with the Primeys aren't even slightly interested in the imminent collapse of civilization! Oh, well. The point is that in the present political picture, you sink with us. Recognizing this, my people are prepared to forget a great deal and document you back into respectability. How about it?'

'Funny,' Hebster said thoughtfully. 'It can't be knowledge that makes miracle-workers out of fairly sober scientists. They all start shooting lightnings at their families and water out of rocks far too early in Primacy to have had time to learn new techniques. It's as if by merely coming close enough to the Aliens to grovel, they immediately move into position to tap a series of cosmic laws more basic than cause and effect.'

The SIC man's face slowly deepened into purple. 'Well, are you coming in, or aren't you? Remember Hebster, in these times, a man who insists on business as usual is a traitor to history.'

'I think Kleimbocher *is* the end,' Hebster nodded to himself. 'Not much point in chasing Alien mentality if you're going to lose your best men on the way. I say let's forget all this nonsense of trying to live as equals in the same universe with Aliens. Let's concentrate on human problems and be grateful that they don't come into our major population centers and tell us to shove over.'

The telephone rang. Braganza had dropped back into his swivel chair. He let the instrument squeeze out several piercing sonic bubbles while he clicked his strong square teeth and maintained a carefully focused glare at his visitor. Finally, he picked it up, and gave it the verbal minima:

'Speaking. He is here. I'll tell him. 'Bye.'

He brought his lips together, kept them pursed for a moment and then, abruptly, swung around to face the window.

'Your office, Hebster. Seems your wife and son are in town and have to see you on business. She the one you divorced ten years ago?'

Hebster nodded at his back and rose once more. 'Probably wants her semi-annual alimony dividend bonus. I'll have to go. Sonia never does office morale any good.'

This meant trouble, he knew. 'Wife-and-son' was executive code for something seriously wrong with Hebster Securities, Inc. He had not seen his wife since she had been satisfactorily maneuvered into giving him control of his son's education. As far as he was concerned, she had earned a substantial income for life by providing him with a well-mothered heir.

'Listen!' Braganza said sharply as Hebster reached the door. He still kept his eyes studiously on the street. 'I tell you this: You don't want to come in with us. All right! You're a businessman first and a world citizen second. All right! But keep your nose clean, Hebster. If we catch you the slightest bit off base from now on, you'll get hit with everything. We'll not only pull the most spectacular trial this corrupt old planet has ever seen, but somewhere along the line, we'll throw you and your entire organization to the wolves. We'll see to it that *Humanity First* pulls the Hebster Tower down around your ears.'

Hebster shook his head, licked his lips. '*Why?* What would that accomplish?'

'Hah! It would give a lot of us here the craziest kind of pleasure. But it would also relieve us temporarily of some of the mass pressure we've been feeling. There's always the chance that Dempsey would lose control of his hotter heads, that they'd go on a real gory rampage, make with the sound and the fury sufficiently to justify full deployment of troops. We could knock off Dempsey and all of the big-shot Firsters then, because John Q. United Mankind would have seen to his own vivid satisfaction and injury what a dangerous mob they are.'

'This,' Hebster commented bitterly, 'is the idealistic, legalistic world government!'

Braganza's chair spun around to face Hebster and his fist

136

came down on the desk top with all the crushing finality of a magisterial gavel. 'No, it is not! It is the SIC, a plenipotentiary and highly practical bureau of the UM, especially created to organize a relationship between Alien and human. Furthermore, it's the SIC in a state of the greatest emergency when the reign of law and world government may topple at a demagogue's belch. Do you think' – his head snaked forward belligerently, his eyes slitted to thin lines of purest contempt – 'that the career and fortune, even the life, let us say, of as openly selfish a slug as you, Hebster, would be placed above that of the representative body of two billion *socially* operating human beings ?'

The SIC official thumped his sloppily buttoned chest. 'Braganza, I tell myself now, you're lucky he's too hungry for his blasted profit to take you up on that offer. Think how much fun it's going to be to sink a hook into him when he makes a mistake at last! To drop him onto the back of *Humanity First* so that they'll run amuck and destroy themselves! Oh, get out, Hebster. I'm through with you.'

He had made a mistake, Hebster reflected as he walked out of the armory and snapped his fingers at a gyrocab. The SIC was the most powerful single government agency in a Primey-infested world; offending them for a man in his position was equivalent to a cab driver delving into the more uncertain aspects of a traffic cop's ancestry in the policeman's popeyed presence.

But what could he do ? Working with the SIC would mean working under Braganza – and since maturity, Algernon Hebster had been quietly careful to take orders from no man. It would mean giving up a business which, with a little more work and a little more time, might somehow still become the dominant combine on the planet. And worst of all, it would mean acquiring a social orientation to replace the calculating businessman's viewpoint which was the closest thing to a soul he had ever known.

The doorman of his building preceded him at a rapid pace down the side corridor that led to his private elevator and flourished aside for him to enter. The car stopped on the twenty-third floor. With a heart that had sunk so deep as to have practically foundered, Hebster picked his way along the wide-eyed clerical stares that lined the corridor. At the entrance to General Laboratory 23B, two tall men in the gray livery of his personal bodyguard moved apart to let him enter. If they had been recalled after having been told to take the day off, it meant that a full-dress emergency was being observed. He hoped that it had been declared in time to prevent any publicity leakage.

It had, Greta Seidenheim assured him. 'I was down here applying the clamps five minutes after the fuss began. Floors, twenty-one through twenty-five are closed off and all outside lines are being monitored. You can keep your employees an hour at most past five o'clock – which gives you a maximum of two hours and fourteen minutes.'

He followed her green-tipped fingernail to the far corner of the lab where a body lay wrapped in murky rags. Theseus. Protruding from his back was the yellowed ivory handle of quite an old German S.S. dagger, 1942 edition. The silver swastika on the hilt had been replaced by an ornate symbol – an HF. Blood had soaked Theseus' long matted hair into an ugly red rug.

A dead Primey, Hebster thought, staring down hopelessly. In *his* building, in the laboratory to which the Primey had been spirited two or three jumps ahead of Yost and Funatti. This was capital offense material – if the courts ever got a chance to weigh it.

'Look at the dirty Primey-lover!' a slightly familiar voice jeered on his right. 'He's scared! Make money out of *that*, Hebster!'

The corporation president strolled over to the thin man with the knobby, completely shaven head who was tied to an unused steampipe. The man's tie, which hung outside his laboratory smock, sported an unusual ornament about halfway down. It took Hebster several seconds to identify it. A miniature gold safety razor upon a black '3'.

'He's a third echelon official of *Humanity First !*'

'He's also Charlie Verus of Hebster Laboratories,' an extremely short man with a corrugated forehead told him. 'My name is Margritt, Mr. Hebster, Dr. J. H. Margritt. I spoke to you on the communicator when the Primeys arrived.'

Hebster shook his head determinedly. He waved back the other scientists who were milling around him self-consciously. 'How long have third echelon officials, let alone ordinary members of *Humanity First*, been receiving salary checks in my laboratories?'

'I don't know.' Margritt shrugged up at him. 'Theoretically, no Firsters can be Hebster employees. Personnel is supposed to be twice as efficient as the SIC when it comes to sifting background. They probably are. But what can they do when an employee joins *Humanity First after* he's passed his probationary period? These proselyting times you'd need a complete force of secret police to keep tabs on all the new converts!'

'When I spoke to you earlier in the day, Margritt, you indicated disapproval of Verus. Don't you think it was your duty to let me know I had a Firster about to mix it up with Primeys?'

The little man beat a violent negative back and forth with his chin. 'I'm paid to supervise research, Mr. Hebster, not to coordinate your labor relations nor vote your political ticket!'

Contempt – the contempt of the creative researcher for the businessman-entrepreneur who paid his salary and was now in serious trouble – flickered behind every word he spoke. Why, Hebster wondered irritably, did people so despise a man who made money? Even the Primeys back in his office, Yost and Funatti, Braganza, Margritt – who had worked in his laboratories for years. It was his only talent. Surely, as such, it was as valid as a pianist's?

'I've never liked Charlie Verus,' the lab chief went on, 'but we never had reason to suspect him of Firstism! He must have hit the third echelon rank about a week ago, eh, Bert?'

'Yeah,' Bert agreed from across the room. 'The day he came in an hour late, broke every Florence flask in the place and told us all dreamily that one day we might be very proud to tell our grandchildren that we'd worked in the same lab with Charles Bolop Verus.'

'Personally,' Margritt commented, 'I thought he might have just finished writing a book which proved that the Great Pyramid was nothing more than a prophecy in stone of our modern textile designs. Verus was that kind. But it probably was his little safety razor that tossed him up so high. I'd say he got the promotion as a sort of payment in advance for the job he finally did today.'

Hebster ground his teeth at the carefully hairless captive who tried, unsuccessfully, to spit in his face; he hurried back to the door where his private secretary was talking to the bodyguard who had been on duty in the lab.

Beyond them, against the wall, stood Larry and S. S. Lusitania conversing in a low-voiced and anxious gabble-honk. They were evidently profoundly disturbed. S. S. Lusitania kept plucking tiny little elephants out of her rags which, kicking and trumpeting tinnily, burst like malformed bubbles as she dropped them on the floor. Larry scratched his tangled beard nervously as he talked, periodically waving a hand at the ceiling which was already studded with fifty or sixty replicas of the dagger buried in Theseus. Hebster couldn't help thinking anxiously of what could have happened to his building if the Primeys had been able to act human enough to defend themselves.

'Listen, Mr. Hebster,' the bodyguard began, 'I was told not to –'

'Save it,' Hebster rapped out. 'This wasn't your fault. Even Personnel isn't to blame, Me and my experts deserve to have our necks chopped for falling so far behind the times. We can analyze any trend but the one which will make us superfluous. Greta! I want my roof helicopter ready to fly and my personal stratojet at LaGuardia alerted. Move, girl! And *you* ... Williams is it?' he queried, leaning forward to read the bodyguard's name on his badge, 'Williams, pack these two Primeys into my helicopter upstairs and stand by for a fast take-off.'

He turned. 'Everyone else!' he called. 'You will be allowed to go home at six. You will be paid one hour's overtime. Thank you.'

Charlie Verus started to sing as Hebster left the lab. By the time he reached the elevator, several of the clerks in the hall-way had defiantly picked up the hymn. Hebster paused outside the elevator as he realized that fully one-fourth of the clerical personnel, male and female, were following Verus' cracked and mournful but terrible earnest tenor.

> *Mine eyes have seen the coming of the glory of the shorn!*
> *We will overturn the cess-pool where the Primey slime is born,*
> *We'll be wearing cleanly garments as we face a human morn –*
> *The First are on the march !*
> *Glory, glory, hallelujah,*
> *Glory, glory, hallelujah . . .*

If it was like this in Hebster Securities, he thought wryly as he came into his private office, how fast was *Humanity First* growing among the broad masses of people ? Of course, many of those singing could be put down as sympathizers rather than converts, people who were suckers for choral groups and vigilante posses – but how much more momentum did an organization have to generate to acquire the name of political juggernaut ?

The only encouraging aspect was the SIC's evident aware-ness of the danger and the unprecedented steps they were prepared to take as countermeasure.

Unfortunately, the unprecedented steps would take place upon Hebster.

He now had a little less than two hours, he reflected, to squirm out of the most serious single crime on the books of present World Law.

He lifted one of his telephones. 'Ruth,' he said. 'I want to speak to Vandermeer Dempsey. Get me through to him personally.'

She did. A few moments later he heard the famous voice, as rich and slow and thick as molten gold. 'Hello Hebster, Vandermeer Dempsey speaking.' He paused as if to draw breath, then went on sonorously: '*Humanity – may it always be ahead, but, ahead or behind, Humanity !*' He chuckled. 'Our newest. What we call our telephone toast. Like it ?'

'Very much,' Hebster told him respectfully, remembering that this former video quizmaster might shortly be church and state combined. 'Er ... Mr. Dempsey, I notice you have a new book out, and I was wondering –'

'Which one ? "Anthropolitics" ?'

'That's it. A fine study! You have some very quotable lines in the chapter headed, "Neither More Nor Less Human".'

A raucous laugh that still managed to bubble heavily. 'Young man, I have quotable lines in every chapter of every book! I maintain a writer's assembly line here at headquarters that is capable of producing up to fifty-five memorable epigrams on any subject upon ten minutes' notice. Not to mention their capacity for political metaphors and two-line jokes with sexy implications! But you wouldn't be calling me to discuss literature, however good a job of emotional engineering I have done in my little text. What is it about, Hebster ? Go into your pitch.'

'Well,' the executive began, vaguely comforted by the Firster chieftain's cynical approach and slightly annoyed at the openness of his contempt, 'I had a chat today with your friend and my friend, P. Braganza.'

'I know.'

'You do ? How ?'

Vandermeer Dempsey laughed again, the slow, good-natured chortle of a fat man squeezing the curves out of a rocking chair. 'Spies, Hebster, *spies*. I have them everywhere practically. This kind of politics is twenty per cent espionage, twenty per cent organization and sixty per cent waiting for the right moment. My spies tell me everything you do.'

'They didn't by any chance tell you what Braganza and I discussed ?'

'Oh, they did, young man, they did!' Dempsey chuckled a carefree scale exercise. Hebster remembered his pictures: the head like a soft and enormous orange, gouged by a brilliant smile. There was no hair anywhere on the head – all of it, down to the last eyelash and follicle wart, was removed regularly through electrolysis. 'According to my agents, Braganza made several strong representations on behalf of the

Special Investigating Commission which you rightly spurned. Then, somewhat out of sorts, he announced that if you were henceforth detected in the nefarious enterprises which everyone knows have made you one of the wealthiest men on the face of the Earth, he would use you as bait for our anger. I must say I admire the whole ingenious scheme immensely.'

'And you're not going to bite,' Hebster suggested. Greta Seidenheim entered the office and made a circular gesture at the ceiling. He nodded.

'On the contrary, Hebster, we *are* going to bite. We're going to bite with just a shade more vehemence that we're expected to. We're going to swallow this provocation that the SIC is devising for us and go on to make a world-wide revolution out of it. We *will*, my boy.'

Hebster rubbed his left hand back and forth across his lips. 'Over my dead body!' He tried to chuckle himself and managed only to clear his throat. 'You're right about the conversation with Braganza, and you may be right about how you'll do when it gets down to paving stones and baseball bats. But, if you'd like to have the whole thing a lot easier, there is a little deal I have in mind –'

'Sorry, Hebster my boy. No deals. Not on this. Don't you see we really *don't* want to have it easier? For the same reason, we pay our spies nothing despite the risks they run and the great growing wealth of *Humanity First*. We found that the spies we acquired through conviction worked harder and took many more chances than those forced into our arms by economic pressure. No, we desperately need *L'affaire Hebster* to inflame the populace. We need enough excitement running loose so that it transmits to the gendarmerie and the soldiery, so that conservative citizens who normally shake their heads at a parade will drop their bundles and join the rape and robbery. Enough such citizens and Terra goes *Humanity First*.'

'Heads you win, tails I lose.'

The liquid gold of Dempsey's laughter poured. 'I see what you mean, Hebster. Either way, UM or HF, you wind up a smear-mark on the sands of time. You had your chance when we asked for contributions from public-spirited businessmen four years ago. Quite a few of your competitors were able to see the valid relationship between economics and politics. Woodran of the Underwood Investment Trust is a first echelon official today. Not a single one of *your* top executives wears a razor. But, even so, whatever happens to you will be mild compared to the Primeys.'

'The Aliens may object to their body-servants being mauled.'

'There are no Aliens!' Dempsey replied in a completely altered voice. He sounded as if he had stiffened too much to be able to move his lips.

'No Aliens? Is that your latest line? You don't mean that!'

'There are only Primeys – creatures who have resigned from human responsibility and are therefore able to do many seemingly miraculous things, which real humanity refuses to do because of the lack of dignity involved. But there are no Aliens. Aliens are a Primey myth.'

Hebster grunted. 'That is the ideal way of facing an unpleasant fact. Stare right through it.'

'If you insist on talking about such illusions as Aliens,' the rustling and angry voice cut in, 'I'm afraid we can't continue the conversation. You're evidently going Prime, Hebster.'

The line went dead.

Hebster scraped a finger inside the mouthpiece rim. 'He believes his own stuff!' he said in an awed voice. 'For all of the decadent urbanity, he has to have the same reassurance he gives his followers – the horrible, superior thing just isn't there!'

Greta Seidenheim was waiting at the door with his briefcase and both their coats. As he came away from the desk, he said, 'I won't tell you not to come along, Greta, but –'

'Good,' she said, swinging along behind him. 'Think we'll make it to – wherever we're going?'

'Arizona. The first and largest Alien settlement. The place our friends with the funny names come from.'

'What can you do there that you can't do here?'

'Frankly, Greta, I don't know. But it's a good idea to lose myself for a while. Then again, I want to get in the area where all this agony originates and take a close look. I'm an off-the-cuff businessman; I've done all of my important figuring on the spot.'

There was bad news waiting for them outside the helicopter. 'Mr. Hebster,' the pilot told him tonelessly while cracking a dry stick of gum, 'the stratojet's been seized by the SIC. Are we still going ? If we do it in this thing, it won't be very far or very fast.'

'We're still going,' Hebster said after a moment's hesitation.

They climbed in. The two Primeys sat on the floor in the rear, sneezing conversationally at each other. Williams waved respectfully at his boss. 'Gently as lambs,' he said. 'In fact, they made one. I had to throw it out.'

The large pot-bellied craft climbed up its rope of air and started forward from the Hebster Building.

'There must have been a leak,' Greta muttered angrily. 'They heard about the dead Primey. Somewhere in the organization there's a leak that I haven't been able to find. The SIC heard about the dead Primey and now they're hunting us down. Real efficient, I am!'

Hebster smiled at her grimly. She *was* very efficient. So was Personnel and a dozen other subdivisions of the organization. So was Hebster himself. But these were functioning members of a normal business designed for stable times. *Political* spies! If Dempsey could have spies and saboteurs all over Hebster Securities, why couldn't Braganza ? They'd catch him before he had even started running; they'd bring him back before he could find a loophole.

They'd bring him back for trial, perhaps, for what in all probability would be known to history as the Bloody Hebster Incident. The incident that had precipitated a world revolution.

'Mr. Hebster, they're getting restless,' Williams called out. 'Should I relax 'em out, kind off ?'

Hebster sat up sharply, hopefully. 'No,' he said. 'Leave them alone!' He watched the suddenly agitated Primeys very closely. This was the odd chance for which he'd brought them along! Years of haggling with Primeys had taught him a lot about them. They were good for other things than sheer gimmick-craft.

Two specks appeared on the windows. They enlarged sleekly into jets with SIC insignia.

'Pilot!' Hebster called, his eyes on Larry who was pulling painfully at his beard. 'Get away from the controls! Fast! Did you hear me? That was an *order! Get away from those controls!*'

The man moved off reluctantly. He was barely in time. The control board dissolved into rattling purple shards behind him. The vanes of the gyro seemed to flower into indigo saxophones. Their ears rang with supersonic frequencies as they rose above the jets on a spout of unimaginable force.

Five seconds later they were in Arizona.

They piled out of their weird craft into a sage-cluttered desert.

'I don't ever want to know what my windmill was turned into,' the pilot commented, 'or what was used to push it along – but how did the Primey come to understand the cops were after us?'

'I don't think he knew that,' Hebster explained, 'but he was sensitive enough to know he was going home, and that somehow those jets were there to prevent it. And so he functioned, in terms of his interests, in what was almost a human fashion. He protected himself!'

'Going home,' Larry said. He'd been listening very closely to Hebster, dribbling from the right-hand corner of his mouth as he listened. 'Haemostat, hammersdarts, hump. Home is where the hate is. Hit is where the hump is. Home and locks the door.'

S.S. Lusitania had started on one leg and favored them with her peculiar fleshy smile. 'Hindsight,' she suggested archly, 'is no more than home site. Gabble, honk?'

Larry started after her, some three feet off the ground. He walked the air slowly and painfully as if the road he traveled were covered with numerous small boulders, all of them pitilessly sharp.

'Good-bye, people,' Hebster said. 'I'm off to see the wizard with my friends in greasy gray here. Remember, when the SIC catches up to your unusual vessel – stay close to it for that purpose, by the way – it might be wise to refer to me as someone who forced you into this. You can tell them I've gone into the wilderness looking for a solution, figuring that if I went Prime I'd still be better off than as a punching bag whose ownership is being hotly disputed by such characters as P. Braganza and Vandermeer Dempsey. I'll be back with my mind or on it.'

He patted Greta's cheek on the wet spot; then he walked deftly away in pursuit of S.S. Lusitania and Larry. He glanced back once and smiled as he saw them looking curiously forlorn, especially Williams, the chunky young man who earned his living by guarding other people's bodies.

The Primeys followed a route of sorts, but it seemed to have been designed by someone bemused by the motions of an accordion. Again and again it doubled back upon itself, folded across itself, went back a hundred yards and started all over again.

This was Primey country – Arizona, where the first and largest Alien settlement had been made. There were mighty few humans in this corner of the southwest any more – just the Aliens and their coolies.

'Larry,' Hebster called as an uncomfortable thought struck him. 'Larry! Do . . . do your masters know I'm coming?'

Missing his step as he looked up at Hebster's peremptory question, the Primey tripped and plunged to the ground. He rose, grimaced at Hebster and shook his head. 'You are not a businessman,' he said. 'Here there can be no business. Here there can only be humorous what-you-might-call-worship. The movement to the universal, the inner nature – The realization, complete and eternal, of the partial and evanescent that alone enables . . . that alone enables –' His clawed fingers writhed into each other, as if he were desperately trying to pull a communicable meaning out of the palms. He shook his head with a slow rolling motion from side to side.

Hebster saw with a shock that the old man was crying. Then going Prime had yet another similarity to madness! It gave the human an understanding of something thoroughly beyond himself, a mental summit he was constitutionally incapable of mounting. It gave him a glimpse of some psychological promised land, then buried him, still yearning, in his own inadequacies. And it left him at last bereft of pride in his realizable accomplishments with a kind of myopic half-knowledge of where he wanted to go but with no means of getting there.

'When I first came,' Larry was saying haltingly, his eyes squinting into Hebster's face, as if he knew what the businessman was thinking, 'when first I tried to know . . . I mean the charts and textbooks I carried here, my statistics, my plotted curves were so useless. All playthings I found, disorganized, based on shadow-thought. And then, Hebster, to watch real-thought, real-control! You'll see the joy – You'll serve beside us, you will! Oh, the enormous lifting –'

His voice died into angry incoherencies as he bit into his fist. S.S. Lusitania came up, still hopping on one foot. 'Larry,' she suggested in a very soft voice, 'gabble-honk Hebster away?'

He looked surprised, then nodded. The two Primeys linked arms and clambered laboriously back up to the invisible road from which Larry had fallen. They stood facing him for a moment, looking like a weird, ragged, surrealistic version of Tweedledee and Tweedledum.

Then they disappeared and darkness fell around Hebster as if it had been knocked out of a jar. He felt under himself cautiously and sat down on the sand which retained all the heat of daytime Arizona.

Now!

Suppose an Alien came. Suppose an Alien asked him point-blank what it was that he wanted. That would be bad. Algernon Hebster, businessman extraordinary – slightly on the run, at the moment, of course – didn't know what he wanted; not with reference to Aliens.

He didn't want them to leave, because the Primey technology he had used in over a dozen industries was essentially an interpretation and adaptation of Alien methods. He didn't want them to stay because whatever was orderly in his world was dissolving under the acids of their omnipresent superiority.

He also knew that he personally did not want to go Prime.

What was left then? Business? Well, that was Braganza's question. What does a businessman do when demand is so well controlled that it can be said to have ceased to exist?

Or what does he do in a case like the present, when demand might be said to be nonexistent, since there was nothing the Aliens seemed to want of Man's puny hoard?

'He *finds* something they want,' Hebster said out loud.

How? *How?* Well, the Indian still sold his decorative blankets to the paleface as a way of life, as a source of income. And he insisted on being paid in cash – not firewater. If *only*, Hebster thought, he could somehow contrive to meet an Alien – he'd find out soon enough what its needs were, what was basically desired.

And then as the retort-shaped, the tube-shaped, the bell-shaped bottles materialized all around him, he understood! They had been forming the insistent questions in his mind. And they weren't satisfied with the answer he had found thus far. They liked answers. They liked answers very much indeed. If he was interested, there was always a way –

A great dots-in-bottle brushed his cortex and he screamed. 'No! I don't *want* to!' he explained desperately.

Ping! went the dots-in-bottles and Hebster grabbed at his body. His continuing flesh reassured him. He felt very much like the girl in Greek mythology who had begged Zeus for the privilege of seeing him in the full regalia of his godhood. A few moments after her request had been granted, there had been nothing left of the inquisitive female but a fine feathery ash.

The bottles were swirling in and out of each other in a strange and intricate dance from which there radiated emotions vaguely akin to curiosity, yet partaking of amusement and rapture.

Why rapture? Hebster was positive he had caught that note,

even allowing for the lack of similarity between mental patterns. He ran a hurried dragnet through his memory, caught a few corresponding items and dropped them after a brief, intensive examination. What was he trying to remember – what was his supremely efficient businessman's instinct trying to remind him of?

The dance became more complex, more rapid. A few bottles had passed under his feet and Hebster could see them, undulating and spinning some ten feet below the surface of the ground as if their presence had made the Earth a transparent as well as permeable medium. Completely unfamiliar with all matters Alien as he was, not knowing – nor caring! – whether they danced as an expression of the counsel they were taking together, or as a matter of necessary social ritual, Hebster was able none the less to sense an approaching climax. Little crooked lines of green lightning began to erupt between the huge bottles. Something exploded near his left ear. He rubbed his face fearfully and moved away. The bottles followed, maintaining him in the imprisoning sphere of their frenzied movements.

Why *rapture*? Back in the city, the Aliens had had a terribly studious air about them as they hovered, almost motionless, above the works and lives of mankind. They were cold and careful scientists and showed not the slightest capacity for . . . for –

So he had something. At last he had something. But what do you do with an idea when you can't communicate it and can't act upon it yourself?

Ping!

The previous invitation was being repeated, more urgently. *Ping! Ping! Ping!*

'No!' he yelled and tried to stand. He found he couldn't. 'I'm not . . . I don't want to go Prime!'

There was detached, almost divine laughter.

He felt that awful scrabbling inside his brain as if two or three entities were jostling each other within it. He shut his eyes hard and thought. He was close, he was very close. He had an idea, but he needed time to formulate it – a little while to figure out just exactly what the idea was and just exactly what to do with it!

Ping, ping, ping! Ping, ping, ping!

He had a headache. He felt as if his mind were being sucked out of his head. He tried to hold on to it. He couldn't.

All right, then. He relaxed abruptly, stopped trying to protect himself. But with his mind and his mouth, he yelled. For the first time in his life and with only a partially formed conception of whom he was addressing the desperate call to, Algernon Hebster screamed for help.

'I can do it!' he alternately screamed and thought. 'Save money, save time, save whatever it is you want to save, whoever you are and whatever you call yourself – I can help you save! Help me, *help me – We* can do it – but *hurry*. Your problem can be solved – Economize. The balance-sheet – *Help –*'

The words and frantic thoughts spun in and out of each other like the contracting rings of Aliens all around him. He kept screaming, kept the focus on his mental images, while, unbearably, somewhere inside him, a gay and jocular force began to close a valve on his sanity.

Suddenly, he had absolutely no sensation. Suddenly, he knew dozens of things he had never dreamed he could know and had forgotten a thousand times as many. Suddenly, he felt that every nerve in his body was under control of his forefinger. Suddenly, he –

Ping, ping, ping! Ping! Ping! PING! PING! PING! PING!

'. . . Like that,' someone said.

'What, for example?' someone else asked.

'Well, they don't even lie normally. He's been sleeping like a human being. They twist and moan in their sleep, the Primeys do, for all the world like habitual old drunks. Speaking of moans, here comes our boy.'

Hebster sat up on the army cot, rattling his head. The fears were leaving him, and, with the fears gone, he would no longer be hurt. Braganza, highly concerned and unhappy, was standing next to his bed with a man who was obviously a doctor.

Hebster smiled at both of them, manfully resisting the temptation to drool out a string of nonsense syllables.

'Hi, fellas,' he said. 'Here I come, ungathering nuts in May.'

'You don't mean to tell me you communicated!' Braganza yelled. 'You communicated and didn't go Prime!'

Hebster raised himself on an elbow and glanced out past the tent flap to where Greta Seidenheim stood on the other side of a port-armed guard. He waved his fist at her, and she nodded a wide-open smile back.

'Found me lying in the desert like a waif, did you?'

'*Found* you!' Braganza spat. 'You were brought in by Primeys, man. First time in history they ever did that. We've been waiting for you to come to in the serene faith that once you did, everything would be all right.'

The corporation president rubbed his forehead. 'It will be, Braganza, it will be. Just Primeys, eh? No Aliens helping them?'

'*Aliens?*' Braganza swallowed. 'What led you to believe – What gave you reason to hope that . . . that *Aliens* would help the Primeys bring you in?'

'Well, perhaps I shouldn't have used the word "help". But I did think there would be a few Aliens in the group that escorted my unconscious body back to you. Sort of an honor guard, Braganza. It would have been a real nice gesture, don't you think?'

The SIC man looked at the doctor who had been following the conversation with interest. 'Mind stepping out for a minute?' he suggested.

He walked behind the man and dropped the tent flap into place. Then he came around to the foot of the army cot and pulled on his mustache vigorously. 'Now, see here, Hebster, if you keep up this clowning, so help me I will slit your belly open and snap your intestines back in your face! *What happened?*'

'What happened?' Hebster laughed and stretched slowly, carefully, as if he were afraid of breaking the bones of his arm. 'I don't think I'll ever be able to answer that question completely. And there's a section of my mind that's very glad that

I won't. This much I remember clearly: I had an idea. I communicated it to the proper and interested party. We concluded – this party and I – a tentative agreement as agents, the exact terms of the agreement to be decided by our principals and its complete ratification to be contingent upon their acceptance. Furthermore, we – All right, Braganza, all right! I'll tell it straight. Put down that folding chair. Remember, I've just been through a pretty unsettling experience!'

'Not any worse than the world is about to go through,' the official growled. 'While you've been out on your three-day vacation, Dempsey's been organizing a full-dress revolution every place at once. He's been very careful to limit it to parades and verbal fireworks so that we haven't been able to make with the riot squads, but it's pretty evident that he's ready to start using muscle. Tomorrow might be it; he's spouting on a world-wide video hookup and it's the opinion of the best experts we have available that his tag line will be the signal for action. Know what their slogan is? It concerns Verus who's been indicted for murder; they claim he'll be a martyr.'

'And you were caught with your suspicions down. How many SIC men turned out to be Firsters?'

Braganza nodded. 'Not too many, but more than we expected. More than we could afford. He'll do it, Dempsey will, unless you've hit the real thing. Look, Hebster,' his heavy voice took on a pleading quality, 'don't play with me any more. Don't hold my threats against me; there was no personal animosity in them, just a terrible, fearful worry over the world and its people and the government I was supposed to protect. If you still have a gripe against me, I, Braganza, give you leave to take it out of my hide as soon as we clear this mess up. But let me know where we stand first. A lot of lives and a lot of history depend on what you did out there in that patch of desert.'

Hebster told him. He began with the extraterrestrial *Walpurgis Nacht*. 'Watching the Aliens slipping in and out of each other in that cock-eyed and complicated rhythm, it struck me how different they were from the thoughtful dots-in-bottles hovering over our busy places, how different all creatures are in their home environments – and how hard it is to get to know them on the basis of their company manners. And then I realized that this place wasn't their home.'

'Of course. Did you find out which part of the galaxy they come from?'

'That's not what I mean. Simply because we have marked this area off – and others like it in the Gobi, in the Sahara, in Central Australia – as a reservation for those of our kind whose minds have crumbled under the clear, conscious and certain knowledge of inferiority, we cannot assume that the Aliens around whose settlements they have congregated have necessarily settled themselves.'

'*Huh?*' Braganza shook his head rapidly and batted his eyes.

'In other words we had made an assumption on the basis of the Aliens' very evident superiority to ourselves. But that assumption – and therefore that superiority – was in our own terms of what is superior and inferior, and not the Aliens'. And it especially might not apply to those Aliens on . . . the reservation.'

The SIC man took a rapid walk around the tent. He beat a great fist into an open sweaty palm. 'I'm beginning to, just beginning to –'

'That's what I was doing at that point, just beginning to. Assumptions that don't stand up under the structure they're supposed to support have caused the ruin of more close-thinking businessmen than I would like to face across any conference table. The four brokers, for example, who, after the market crash of 1929 –'

'All right,' Braganza broke in hurriedly, taking a chair near the cot. 'Where did you go from there?'

'I still couldn't be certain of anything; all I had to go on were a few random thoughts inspired by extra-substantial adrenalin secretions and, of course, the strong feeling that these particular Aliens weren't acting the way I had become accustomed to expect Aliens to act. They reminded me of something, of somebody. I was positive that once I got that memory tagged, I'd have most of the problem solved. And I was right.'

'How were you right? What was the memory?'

'Well, I hit it backwards, kind of. I went back to Professor Kleimbocher's analogy about the paleface inflicting firewater on the Indian. I've always felt that somewhere in that analogy was the solution. And suddenly, thinking of Professor Kleimbocher and watching those powerful creatures writhing their way in and around each other, suddenly I knew what was wrong. Not the analogy, but our way of using it. We'd picked it up by the hammer head instead of the handle. The paleface gave firewater to the Indian all right – but he got something in return.'

'What?'

'Tobacco. Now there's nothing very much wrong with tobacco if it isn't misused, but the first white men to smoke probably went as far overboard as the first Indians to drink. And both booze and tobacco have this in common – they make you awfully sick if you use too much for your initial experiment. See, Braganza? These Aliens out here in the desert reservation are *sick*. They have hit something in our culture that is as psychologically indigestible to them as . . . well, whatever they have that sticks in our mental gullet and causes ulcers among us. They've been put into a kind of isolation in our desert areas until the problem can be licked.'

'Something that's as indigestible psychologically – What could it be, Hebster?'

The businessman shrugged irritably. 'I don't know. And I don't want to know. Perhaps it's just that they can't let go of a problem until they've solved it – and they can't solve the problems of mankind's activity because of mankind's inherent and basic differences. Simply because we can't understand them, we had no right to assume that they could and did understand us.'

'That wasn't all, Hebster. As the comedians put it – everything we can do, they can do better.'

'Then why did they keep sending Primeys in to ask for those weird gadgets and impossible gimcracks?'

'They could duplicate anything we made.'

'Well, maybe that is it,' Hebster suggested. 'They could

duplicate it, but could they design it? They show every sign of being a race of creatures who never had to make very much for themselves; perhaps they evolved fairly early into animals with direct control over matter, thus never having had to go through the various stages of artifact design. This, in our terms, is a tremendous advantage; but it inevitably would have concurrent disadvantages. Among other things, it would mean a minimum of art forms and a lack of basic engineering knowledge of the artifact itself if not of the directly activated and altered material. The fact is I was right, as I found out later.

'For example. Music is not a function of theoretical harmonics, of complete scores in the head of a conductor or composer – these come later, much later. Music is first and foremost a function of the particular instrument, the reed pipe, the skin drum, the human throat – it is a function of tangibles which a race operating upon electrons, positrons and mesons would never encounter in the course of its construction. As soon as I had that, I had the other flaw in the analogy – the assumption itself.'

'You mean the assumption that we are necessarily inferior to the Aliens?'

'Right, Braganza. They can do a lot that we can't do, but vice very much indeed versa. How many special racial talents we possess that they don't is a matter of pure conjecture – and may continue to be for a good long time. Let the theoretical boys worry that one a century from now, just so they stay away from it at present.'

Braganza fingered a button on his green jerkin and stared over Hebster's head. 'No more scientific investigation of them, eh?'

'Well, we can't right now and we have to face up to that mildly unpleasant situation. The consolation is that they have to do the same. Don't you see? It's not a basic inadequacy. We don't have enough facts and can't get enough at the moment through normal channels of scientific observation because of the implicit psychological dangers to both races. Science, my forward-looking friend, is a complex of interlocking theories, *all derived from observation.*

'Remember, long before you had any science of navigation you had coast-hugging and river-hopping traders who knew how the various currents affected their leaky little vessels, who had learned things about the relative dependability of the moon and the stars – without any interest at all in integrating these scraps of knowledge into broader theories. Not until you have a sufficiently large body of these scraps, and are able to distinguish the preconceptions from the actual observations, can you proceed to organize a science of navigation without running the grave risk of drowning while you conduct your definitive experiments.

'A trader isn't interested in theories. He's interested only in selling something that glitters for something that glitters even more. In the process, painlessly and imperceptibly, he picks up bits of knowledge which gradually reduce the area of unfamiliarity. Until one day there are enough bits of knowledge on which to base a sort of preliminary understanding, a working hypothesis. And then, some Kleimbocher of the future, operating in an area no longer subject to the sudden and unexplainable mental disaster, can construct meticulous and exact laws out of the more obviously valid hypotheses.'

'I might have known it would be something like this, if you came back with it, Hebster! So their theorists and our theorists had better move out and the traders move in. Only how do we contact their traders – if they have any such animals ?'

The corporation president sprang out of bed and began dressing. 'They have them. Not a Board of Director type perhaps – but a business-minded Alien. As soon as I realized that the dots-in-bottles were acting, relative to their balanced scientific colleagues, very like our own high IQ Primeys, I knew I needed help. I needed someone I could tell about it, someone on their side who had as great a stake in an operating solution as I did. There had to be an Alien in the picture somewhere who was concerned with profit and loss statements, with how much of a return you get out of a given investment of time, personnel, material and energy. I figured with him I could talk – *business*. The simple approach: What have you got that we want and how little of what we have will you take for it. No attempts to understand completely incompatible philosophies. There had to be that kind of character somewhere in the expedition. So I shut my eyes and let out what I fondly hoped was a telepathic *yip* channeled to him. I was successful.

'Of course, I might not have been successful if he hadn't been searching desperately for just that sort of *yip*. He came buzzing up in a rousing United States Cavalry-routs-the-red-skins type of rescue, stuffed my dripping psyche back into by subconscious and hauled me up into some sort of never-never ship. I've been in this interstellar version of Mohammed's coffin, suspended between Heaven and Earth, for three days, while he alternately bargained with me and consulted the home office about developments.

'We dickered the way I do with Primeys – by running down a list of what each of us could offer and comparing it with what we wanted; each of us trying to get a little more than we gave to the other guy, in our own terms, of course. Buying and selling are intrinsically simple processes; I don't imagine our discussions were very much different from those between a couple of Phoenician sailors and the blue-painted Celtic inhabitants of early Britain.'

'And this . . . this business-Alien never suggested the possibility of taking what they wanted –'

'By force? No, Braganza, not once. Might be they're too civilized for such shenanigans. Personally, I think the big reason is that they don't have any idea of what it is they do want from us. We represent a fantastic enigma to them – a species which uses matter to alter matter, producing objects which, while intended for similar functions, differ enormously from each other. You might say that we ask the question *"how?"* about their activities; and they want to know the *"why?"* about ours. Their investigators have compulsions even greater than ours. As I understand it, the intelligent races they've encountered up to this point are all comprehensible to them since they derive from parallel evolutionary paths. Every time one of their researchers get close to the answer of why we wear various colored clothes even in climates where clothing is unnecessary, he slips over the edges and splashes.

'Of course, that's why this opposite number of mine was so worried. I don't know his exact status – he may be anything from the bookkeeper to the business-manager of the expedition – but it's his bottle-neck if the outfit continues to be un-economic. And I gathered that not only has his occupation kind of barred him from doing the investigation his unstable pals were limping back from into the asylums he's constructed here in the deserts, but those of them who've managed to retain their sanity constantly exhibit a healthy contempt for him. They feel, you see, that their function is that of the expedition. He's strictly supercargo. Do you think it bothers them one bit,' Hebster snorted, 'that he has a report to prepare, to show how his expedition stood up in terms of a balance sheet –'

'Well, you did manage to communicate on that point, at least,' Braganza grinned. 'Maybe traders using the simple, earnestly chiseling approach will be the answer. You've certainly supplied us with more basic data already than years of heavily subsidized research. Hebster, I want you to go on the air with this story you told me and show a couple of Primey Aliens to the video public.'

'Uh-uh. You tell 'em. You can use the prestige. I'll think a message to my Alien buddy along the private channel he's keeping open for me, and he'll send you a couple of human-happy dots-in-bottles for the telecast. I've got to whip back to New York and get my entire outfit to work on a really en-cyclopedic job.'

'Encyclopedic?'

The executive pulled his belt tight and reached for a tie. 'Well, what else would you call the first edition of the Hebster Interstellar Catalogue of all Human Activity and Available Artifacts, prices available upon request with the understanding that they are subject to change without notice?'